BARBARIANS TREASURE

A SCIFI ALIEN ROMANCE NOVEL

RUBY DIXON

Copyright © 2020 by Ruby Dixon

All rights reserved.

No part of this book may be reproduced in any form or by any electronic or mechanical means, including information storage and retrieval systems, without written permission from the author, except for the use of brief quotations in a book review.

Cover Photo: Sara Eirew Photographer

Cover Design: Kati Wilde

Edits: Aquila Editing

❦ Created with Vellum

BARBARIAN'S TREASURE

Everyone knows Megan and Cashol hit it off the moment they resonated...didn't they? But when Josie goes into labor, an offhand comment makes Megan point out to her friend that no, things weren't always so smooth. Just because resonance is immediate doesn't mean it's immediately perfect.

But also...just because it's an instant bond doesn't mean it's wrong. Sometimes it's very, very right.

1

MEGAN

"I am thinking I should go back to the Icehome beach," Cashol says, lying flat in the furs across from the fire one night.

"I think you'll go over my dead body," I say tartly. I macramé another leather-strap rug, my fingers busy weaving. "You just came back."

"Yes, but they will need help getting through the brutal season. You should have seen how terrible they are at surviving." Cashol crooks a grin at me. "Their stews were far worse than yours, and Leezh and Har-loh are the most experienced cooks they have there. You should feel pity for them."

"First of all, Gail is there," I point out. This is a game we play at night, just so Cashol can feel appreciated. He teases me, telling me that he's going to leave my side again and tries to get me all riled up. It worked the first few times, but now it's just an easy game between us, where he needles me and I snap back. He likes it when I'm sassy, apparently, and I get super sassy when I'm pregnant...or when he talks about going back to the beach. Right now, it's both. "And second of all, Brooke is there, too, and she's a decent cook. And thirdly, I will spank the hell out of you if you even so much as think of leaving my side before this baby is born."

"Will you, now?" My incorrigible mate gets a playful look in his eyes. "Perhaps I should threaten this more often if it means you will put your hands all over my tail-side."

"Like you need an excuse to get more groping," I tease. "I barely keep my hands off you as it is."

"Especially my feet—"

Holvek chooses that moment to join us in the cave. "Daddy, my net broke and we're trying to catch more dirtbeaks."

I make another twist in the mat, adding a decorative braid around the edges. This one's for Josie's little house. Her storage area has a particularly cold floor and with this latest pregnancy, she likes to go barefoot thanks to feet swelling, so I'm making her a mat to step on. I'm always making mats for someone, because I like to keep my hands busy. Plus, it helps pass the time, and I've learned that when my hands are busy, my head is less busy.

"Let me see your net, Holvek," Cashol says, and I love that he changes to his dad voice. It turns me on to hear him so authoritative and protective of our son. They bend their heads together and I swear, they're both identical. If I hadn't carried Holvek for a whopping fourteen months in my body, I'd think he's someone else's child and not mine. The only part of him that looks like me are his five wiggly toes to his father's three. The rest is pure sa-khui and a hundred percent Cashol.

I rub my rounded belly and wonder if this next one will look like me or if I'm going to be surrounded by a bunch of Cashol clones for all my life. The thought makes me smile. Not a hardship there.

"I can fix this part," Cashol says, his fingers deftly moving over the loose area of the net. "I am not as good with tying things as your mother but I will do my best." He gives me a sultry look from underneath his brows that even now makes me blush. He is just asking to be spanked. "And I hope you are not hurting the dirtbeaks? We talked about that."

"Masan wants a friend for his," Holvek tells me, his stubborn little mouth quirking. "And I want one, too."

"Noooo," I say with a shake of my head, lowering my mat so I can give my best mom glare to my son. "You know what I said about pets."

"No pets." He looks crestfallen at the thought. "Not even a snowcat?"

"You're going to have a baby sister or baby brother soon." I point at my jutting belly. Even though I'm nowhere close to delivering, my belly feels bigger than the last time I carried, and I fully admit to milking the pregnancy for all its worth. "The last thing we need is a snowcat in the house. You've seen how big Kate's kitten is!"

"It's huuuuge," Holvek tells me with wide eyes. "It's almost as big as I am already. I bet I could ride him."

"You need to stay far away from him," I say. Now I'm going to have mom nightmares of Holvek playing with the cat and the cat eating him. Holvek pouts again, but I shake my head. "No dirtbeaks, no cats. I mean it."

He looks at Cashol.

Cashol looks at me. "We will...talk about it." He pats our son on the arm.

Oh we will, will we? I narrow my eyes at the two of them. Are they plotting for pets behind my back? I'm a little hurt that I've been left out of some secret conversation. I love my mate, and I love my boy. I always thought Holvek was a bit of a mama's boy, but if he's got secrets with his dad...I don't know why I'm jealous, just that I am.

Holvek looks at me with an innocent, inquisitive expression. "Mommy, what's groping?"

Oh, so sly. I've been mated to his father for years, and I know a subject change when I see one. Clever little squirt.

Cashol speaks up before I do. "It is what your mother does to your father when she pretends to be mad but secretly wants snuggles." He leans in toward our son. "Mommy thinks that she gets better snuggles that way."

My son giggles. "Does she?"

"Of course not," Cashol straightens, tossing out the newly repaired net. He gives me a clever look. "All of my snuggles are always the best snuggles to be had."

I snort, my sour mood leaving in an instant once more. Count on Cashol to tease me right back to happy. "You just be careful with the dirtbeaks, baby," I tell Holvek. "Come give Mommy a kiss."

He races to my side and flings his little arms around my neck, kissing my cheek with a loud smack. Then, he runs to his father and does the same, and then gathers his net and runs back out the door, yelling for his friends.

I'm left alone with my mate.

Cashol gives me a slow, gorgeous smile that makes my heart flip over in my chest. "So...is it time for snuggles?"

I giggle like a teenage dork, because my big, sprawling alien mate saying "snuggles" is the funniest thing ever. "I don't know. Are you planning on getting a secret pet with our son behind my back? I might not want to snuggle after learning that."

He shrugs, getting on all fours and prowling across the floor of the hut over to my side. He leans in and nips at my neck, fake-growling like an absolute fool and I can't stop smiling. "Masan has a pet. Farli has a pet. Kate has a pet. Our son loves animals. What is so wrong with teaching him about taking care of them as well as hunting them?"

"We talked about this," I say with a tiny sigh, because he's sucking on my earlobe and nuzzling at my neck and I know he's distracting me. It's how he wins arguments. He's too damn good at distractions. "A dirtbeak is dirty and a snowcat is too dangerous."

"Perhaps something, at least?" He nips at my jaw. "Something to keep a growing boy busy and to give his overworked mother some free time?"

"Am I overworked?" I reach up and caress his cheek, leaning into his touch. "I didn't realize."

"So overworked," he agrees. "There is hardly time for Mehgan's poor mate, who suffers greatly from such neglect." I snort, and he kisses my jaw. "It is true," he murmurs, and the tease in his voice makes me smile. "So neglected I have not had a good foot rub in seasons and seasons."

I groan. And the truth comes out. "Is all of this angling so I'll play with your feet?"

"No." He tugs at the neckline of my tunic, revealing my shoulder and kissing his way down. "It is all angling so you can warm my furs *and* play with my feet."

"Lucky me," I tease, but his lips are so skillful that I don't even mind he gets his way.

I DON'T MAKE IT OVER TO JOSIE'S HUT TO DELIVER THE MAT UNTIL later that afternoon, even though I finished it before lunch. I spend far too much time with Cashol, snuggling after all, and then there's a minor emergency when Holvek smashes his finger while dirtbeak hunting and has to have his boo-boos kissed away before going to see the healer. By the time I arrive to visit my friend with the mat, I'm ready for dinner and an early bedtime.

I scratch at the door, inwardly wincing because I can hear the noise from my hut next door. When no one answers, probably because they can't hear me, I pause and then push aside the door flap, peeking in. "Hello?"

Josie's house is, of course, utter chaos. She's only got one more kid than me, but with the noise, you'd think it's twenty. Joha is chewing on one of Josie's bone ladles and banging another against the floor. Joden is running in circles, screaming a song about multiplication tables while Haeden calmly works on lashing together a crib out of bone. Josie is in the middle of the chaos, folding soft leather towels and humming to herself.

My friend looks up at the sight of me, her face lighting up. "Oh! Megan! I didn't hear you knock."

"I figured." Her house is always several decibels louder than everyone else's but Josie never seems to mind. She just beams at me and pats at the empty seat next to her. "Come sit. Haeden, will you make some tea for us, baby?"

"Of course." The big, surly looking hunter gets to his feet immediately and moves to his mate's side. He touches her belly briefly, plants a kiss atop her head, and then moves to the fire. Josie smiles at his back, as in love today as she was when they first resonated. She looks over at me as I sit next to her, and the hard rock seat has a fluffy pillow atop it so it's not as firm on pregnant backsides.

I notice Josie's sitting on one, too, and her belly looks utterly enormous. She's due any week now, with our birth times being harder to pin down thanks to the longer sa-khui gestation. She rubs her back absently as I settle in next to her and offer the rolled mat. "For your kitchen. So it won't be so cold on bare feet."

Her gasp of pleasure is all the payment I need. Josie's eyes shine with excitement and she hugs it to her chest as Haeden moves around the fire. "Oh, Meggers! You shouldn't have!"

"What, I'm going to sit around all day and do nothing? I'm not that pregnant yet." I pat my much smaller belly. "This little one's going to be baking in the oven for a bit longer."

"Plenty of time to think up a good name," Josie teases. "What's Cashol locked onto this week?"

I groan. "This week it's 'Meganash,' I said hell no."

My mate—my sweet, ridiculous, too-lighthearted mate—loves nothing more than to run a joke into the ground, all to make me laugh. When Holvek was about to be born, Cashol tormented me daily with terrible name combinations. Some people's names fit great together—like Georgie and Vektal—but mine and Cashol's? Not so much. There isn't a combination that doesn't make me wince painfully. Cashol knows it, too, which is why he keeps throwing it out there, the nut.

Then again, it always makes me smile.

"I mean, I don't hate it?" Josie wrinkles her nose. "I don't love it but I don't hate it."

"It's a no," I repeat. "A firm no. What about you? Got a name for number three?"

"If it's a girl..." Josie glances over at her mate. "I thought about..." She lowers her voice. "Zalah."

Haeden straightens. "No."

Josie ignores his response. She just smiles at me. "We're talking about it."

Zalah? The woman that Haeden's first cootie resonated to and died? Josie's told me all about it, and I thought she hated the woman. Heck, I thought Haeden did, too. But...I get it. When you're pregnant, you also get sentimental. Josie's probably wanting to honor his first almost-mate in some way. "Maybe as a middle name," I compromise.

"Do sa-khui even have middle names?" She looks surprised.

They don't. Which is kinda the point. I glance over at her surly looking mate, and I'm always surprised at how taciturn Haeden can be such good friends with my playful Cashol. Which reminds me... "Speaking of arguments you can't win, Cashol told Holvek he can have a pet and so now my son is trying to collect a dirtbeak."

"Oh god." Josie gives a shudder of horror. She grabs my arm, because Joden has paused near his father. "Don't say that in his hearing or he's going to want one, too."

Haeden quickly pours two cups of tea and sets them down on a little "table" next to Josie's chair. He puts a fingertip under her chin, tilting her head up for a kiss, and then murmurs to her. "Shall I take the little ones out for a walk?"

She gives him a melting look. "You are the best mate. You know that?"

"I know." He straightens, nods at me, and then scoops up Joha with one arm, and grabs a pile of cloaks with another. "Come, Joden. Let us get some dirtbeak nests for your mother."

"Dirt-beaks!" Joden chants. "Dirt-beaks! Dirt-beaks!"

It's a whirlwind of chaos for the next thirty seconds as Haeden ushers his rambunctious children out the door and then it's just me and Josie. She holds a cup of tea out to me, and when I take it, her hands immediately go to the small of her back. She winces.

I freeze. "Is it time? Should I go stop Haeden?"

Josie waves a hand in the air. "I've got hours yet. Or days. It's just the occasional contraction and a backache, you know? If this is anything like when Joha came, it'll be another day at least before my water breaks. Haeden's ready to get Maylak at a moment's notice, but I told him to wait. So...dirtbeaks, huh?"

"Or a snowcat."

"With a new baby on the way?" She's shocked.

"That's what I said—no way." I'm glad someone's on my side at least. "Sometimes I think he deliberately works me up just to see me riled." I shake my head, smiling wryly at the thought.

"It's so funny how things work," Josie says, shifting her hips with a little grimace. Her hand flutters over her stomach, and I can tell she's feeling something unpleasant, but if she doesn't want to get the healer yet, I'm content to sit here with her and talk. "Haeden and I had such a stormy beginning and now we're pretty much in lock-step about everything." She pauses for a moment. "Well, except the baby's name. But overall, we just agree on everything." Her smile grows. "Meanwhile, you and Cashol had such an easy beginning compared to ours."

I snort. "Are you crazy? Easy?"

My friend looks surprised. "It wasn't?"

"Bitch, no!"

Her eyes widen, and then she giggles. "Bitch, are you lying to me?"

"I remember it very differently than you do, it seems," I say, and then add, "Bitch."

Josie's giggles get louder, and then break off with a little hiss. Her hands clench over her belly for a moment. "That was a definite shift of something." She adjusts herself on her seat again, as if she can't quite get comfortable, and then picks up her tea again. "Okay, well, I seem to recall just you looking over at Cashol one day and squealing with delight—"

"Squealing?" I sputter.

"Squealing, bitch," Josie says solemnly, and then ruins it with more giggles.

I can't help it, I burst into laughter, too.

"And I remember thinking how lucky you were that it was so darn easy," Josie continues. "So if it wasn't easy, then how do you remember it?"

I think for a moment, trying to remember that early time. Maybe Josie remembers it as me finding my happy-ever-after instantly, but it wasn't instant. It might have looked simple, but everything was more complicated. It always is. "You sure you want to hear this story?"

She gestures at her belly. "Like I'm going anywhere?"

She's got a point.

2

EIGHT YEARS AGO

MEGAN

The stack of baskets in my arms wobbles precariously. I chew on my lip, studying how I can possibly carry so much weight in my arms. Josie grabbed the furs, and is trotting the entire unwieldy pile from the storage area over to Hemalo's cave, just as requested. Me, I got stuck with the dye roots, and while it looked like an easy task, I'm quickly realizing I don't have enough hands to carry all of this. My face burns and I fight a ripple of anxiety. Everyone's watching us work, which makes me feel as if I'm on a stage and I'm being judged. Humans are thought of as puny and overly weak, and I'm constantly worried that those of us that aren't pulling our weight are going to be culled from the tribe. That I'm going to somehow be seen as lacking and driven back out into the snow.

No one's said anything like that at all, but I can't help but think it.

After all, we're strangers here. It doesn't matter that we've been here for weeks now, or that Georgie mated with their chief. It doesn't matter that Liz, Nora, Stacy, Ariana and Marlene all resonated immediately and were welcomed into the tribe. The sa-khui people are super nice but their tribe was dying out.

It's very obvious that we're wanted for the fact that we're female and we can have babies.

And it feels like a ticking time bomb over the heads of those of us that haven't resonated. It feels painfully obvious in so many ways. So some of us—Josie and myself in particular—do our best to be helpful. We volunteer for shitty chores, work long hours on scraping furs and helping with food, and we never say "no" to anything that's asked of us.

We're guests here. As long as we're not mated to anyone, that's all we are. Guests.

A guest can quickly overstay their welcome. I think about that all the time, and it makes me fling the baskets of roots on top of one another quickly, determined to carry them all. I know Farli could absolutely carry them, and she's just a kid. I don't want to be seen as more worthless than a child, so I need to suck it up.

I pick up the stack of baskets, and they immediately slide out of my arms and tumble to the ground, scattering their contents.

The cave goes silent, and it feels like everyone is staring at me.

Hot tears prick at the backs of my eyes and I freeze in place. Oh god. I've fucked up. I've fucked up I've fucked up I've fucked up and I can see all the roots mixing with each other and they're on the floor and someone's going to get mad and yell at me and—

"Here. Let me help with that." The voice is thickly accented, but kind, and one of the alien men crouches next to the mess

I've made at the entrance to the storage cave. He picks up the roots with quick, easy motions, as if this is no big deal.

I look around the cave, and no one's looking in our direction anymore. No one's yelling. No one's mad.

My body shuddering, I drop to a crouch and start to scoop up roots, as well. "I'm sorry," I whisper. "I'm sorry. I just..."

"You have puny arms. I know." The alien man chuckles.

I stop, staring at him in shock.

He glances up at me, a teasing sparkle in his strange, glowing blue eyes. The grin on his face is lighthearted and it's clear he's just playing around. I let out a tense breath and relax, just a little. "What, you mean this isn't how you dye the cave floor?"

"It's not," he agrees, grinning. His teeth are bright white, his smile ready. "Besides, if you mix all these colors together, it does not come out like a rainbow."

"Oh no?"

"It comes out the color of dung," he says, tossing them haphazardly into baskets, regardless of where they go. "When I was a kit, I wanted to dye my insides. You can guess the results."

I chuckle at that. "A raging case of food poisoning?"

"That, and the most disappointing dye project ever." He makes a sad face and I can't help but giggle again. His smile grows. "You are Meh-gan, yes?"

I nod, feeling frozen once more. He's flirting with me, and normally I'd flirt back and tease. But relationships are different here. There aren't casual hookups. There aren't bars to hit on strangers or dance floors to dance your cares away in the arms of a one-night stand. There's just a cave that we all live in and a cootie that makes all the decisions, and so I feel like I can't flirt with this man. I just can't.

But he's being so nice.

"It's actually pronounced Meh-*g*an," I correct, emphasizing the hard "g" in the middle that no one ever gets right. Then I immediately feel like an asshole, because why am I correcting him? He learned my language. I'm just the stinking guest. He belongs here. I don't. I'm horrified at my own rudeness, and his expectant look just makes me feel worse. "Um, wh-what did you say your name was again?"

Is that a flicker of disappointment on his face? "I am Cashol."

I feel like such an ass. "Cashol," I repeat, even though I'm sure he's told me his name at least twice. "It's...a lot to learn. I'm sorry. I'm bad with names."

"You only need to learn mine," he says confidently.

I fight the urge to roll my eyes, but I smile at him as he takes the baskets in his arms, as if it was his choice to help me all along. I don't mind the flirting if he helps me not look so pathetic in front of the rest of the tribe. I steal a few glances at him as he helps me stack a few of the baskets into my arms properly, and I assess his looks. He's not the best looking of the barbarians. In fact...he might be the ugliest? Which is unfair, because they're all ridiculously attractive by human standards. They all have fantastic bone structure and strong features, but Cashol also has a big nose that dominates his long face, and a slightly goofy smile that always seems to crease his cheeks. He's appealing, yes, but he's not handsome. His black hair is thick and full, but it's tied back in a messy braid, as if he doesn't give a shit about what he looks like.

He's not my type, I decide. Even if I wanted to flirt, I usually go for pretty men. Somber men. Intense men. Poets and musicians and emo boys who feel the world has failed them. I'm drawn to the drama. But Cashol is nice, and friendly, so I smile at him and thank him for his help.

"If you need anything else, let me know," he says, lingering after he deposits the baskets. Josie's busy leaning over Hemalo's shoulder, trying to learn, so she doesn't notice that Cashol is still here and flirting with me in that awkward, sa-khui way. "I can lift things all day and spare those puny arms."

I arch an eyebrow at him. "Did you ever think that maybe telling me I have puny arms won't get you very far?"

He grins, looking like an utter devil. "No."

I snort with amusement despite myself. His teasing is a nice respite from the constant feeling of uncertainty that's been accompanying me lately.

Cashol keeps standing there, and he rubs his chest. Immediately, my good humor vanishes. Of course he's hoping for resonance, hoping that his khui will light up and start purring now that I'm standing next to him. Inwardly, I cringe even as I keep smiling. Because just that little movement is enough to remind me that I'm valued for my womb above everything else. It's not about Megan. It's about Megan's ability to carry a baby. My safety here depends on me being fertile, and it's utterly terrifying and hurts at the same time.

Back on Earth, I was pregnant. Newly discovered, and newly excited. Sure, I'd be a single mom, but I'd take this on with enthusiasm and I'd love the hell out of my baby so much that it wouldn't matter that there was no dad in the picture. But then the aliens kidnapped me and decided that I'd be more valuable without an occupied womb, and they got rid of my baby like it was nothing.

I still feel as if I'm processing that grief, even as I worry if I'll be able to carry another. I haven't resonated. What if...what if something's wrong with me? What if I never resonate?

Will they still take care of me, these aliens? Will they still share their food and blankets? Look at me with smiles? Or will I be a problem? A burden?

I need answers.

3

CASHOL

I made her smile. Laugh.

I consider this a good thing. All of the human females that have joined our tribe carry sadness in their eyes, but this one in particular intrigues me. She holds herself apart from the others, and for me, it is a challenge to get her to look at me. To smile. She did not know my name when I spoke to her, and that stings a little, but I do not let it keep me down. She knows my name now, and that is all that is important.

I have a jaunty roll in my step as I saunter through the cave.

"You are in a good mood," my friend Haeden comments as I pass by. He sharpens the head of his spear absently, running a sharp rock against the bone edge. "Should I ask why?"

I cross my arms and lean against a nearby wall, even as Vektal approaches and sits with us. "I am in a good mood because I spoke with Meh-gan. I made her smile."

"Is she the noisy one?"

"She is the yellow-haired one that is friends with the noisy one."

Haeden grunts, annoyance flashing over his face. He does not like the noisy one. He thinks she talks far too much. Perhaps she does, but hearing so much happy female chatter is not a bad thing. The caves have been quiet for far too long. Now they are bursting with life, and I am glad for it.

Vektal listens in, saying nothing.

I nod at my chief. "We are allowed to pleasure-mate with the human females, yes? If they are agreeable to it?"

"She has said she wishes to join you in your furs?" Vektal looks surprised.

"No. But I can be convincing." I grin at him. "I like her. I like making her smile." I never thought I would have the opportunity to have a mate of my own. It always seemed a foregone conclusion that if there were any females my age, they would veer toward other members of the tribe, the handsomest ones, or Vektal, who is now the chief. I am just a hunter with an unremarkable face and a good sense of humor. But now that the humans have arrived...there is all kinds of possibility ahead of us.

It is hard not to get attached. To want a female for myself. I am already addicted to Meh-gan's smiles, her laughter. I think about her at night. I think about her when I stroke my cock in private, wondering if someday someone else will do this for me or if I will be forever using my hand.

Not that my hand is not good.

But Meh-gan's hand would be better.

Vektal gets to his feet, a troubled expression on his face. "Come walk with me, Cashol. I would have a word." He walks off, heading for the main cave entrance.

I exchange a troubled look with Haeden, who is equally surprised. I shrug and head after my chief, curious.

I find Vektal pacing out in the snow, his arms crossed over

his chest, tail twitching. He has a grim look on his face, and for a moment, my heart stutters. It feels as if he is going to tell me to pick another female, because Meh-gan has already resonated to another...or that he wants her for himself.

But...my chief is happy with his mate Shorshie, is he not? And when I left Meh-gan's side she was not resonating. So it cannot be that. Even so, I do not like the look on his face. "What troubles you, cousin?"

"I just wish to give you a word of warning in private."

"A word of warning, eh?" I keep a smile on my face even as I step next to my pacing chief. "You are going to tell me not to overwhelm her with my charm?"

Vektal snorts. "I am going to tell you that I do not mind if you court a female, but that particular one, you must go slow. Let her set the pace."

As if I would not? While I can sometimes have the "subtlety of a smoking mountain" as my father Holvek used to say, I would not push Meh-gan into my furs if she had no wish to be there. "Of course not."

"She looks healthy and happy, but she is still healing here." Vektal taps his brow. "Shorshie has told me she endured many bad things when they were held captive by the others. Meh-gan suffered the loss of a kit she carried."

I am stunned. My heart feels as if it has stopped in my chest. "You mean...she already has a mate? A human mate?"

He shakes his head. "From what Georgie has told me, it is different with humans. They do not require resonance to have a kit. Meh-gan had no mate, and her kit was the result of a pleasure-mating. The bad ones stole it from her, and she carries sadness in her heart." He touches my shoulder. "If anyone can ease a sad heart, it is you, cousin, but you must remember that she is fragile. You must go slow with her."

This has given me much to consider. I nod, thoughtful. It has changed nothing about how I feel about Meh-gan. If anything, I am more determined now to be the reason why she smiles each day. But my approach must change. I must be clever, and patient...two things I am not very good at.

I sigh. "I thank you, Vektal. I will remember this and take your advice."

My chief nods and claps my shoulder once more. "I do not mean to discourage you."

"Oh, I am not discouraged." I grin at him. "I do not think a herd of screaming metlaks could discourage me. But you have given me much to think about."

Many, many things to think about.

4

MEGAN

I visit the healer later that day, absolutely positive that she's going to give me bad news. That there's something wrong with my body now, and that I can't carry a baby. That the aliens that got rid of my last one did something to me and that's why I haven't resonated. I brace myself for terrible news, but all I get are gentle smiles and reassuring pats. Maylak doesn't speak English, but even with our limited communication, her answer is obvious.

I'm fine. It just hasn't happened yet.

Which is a relief. I leave the healer's cave feeling better about things...and yet, still worried. I won't relax until I resonate. Until I'm completely secure in my place here. I'm grateful I'm no longer a slave and that I'm "free" here on the ice planet, but at the same time, if these people get tired of me, there's nowhere else to go. So I smile and do more than my fair share of chores. I stay busy at all times, keeping a macramé project in my hands so I always look as if I'm dutifully hard at work.

Who would have thought when I learned how to macramé back in Girl Scouts that I'd end up finding it so damn useful? Yet here I am, macramé-ing as if my life depended on it. Heck, it just might.

The day after I visit the healer, I'm sitting in the "bachelorette" cave with Josie and the others, working on my latest project, when Cashol wanders in, an enormous dead animal slung over his shoulders.

"Did someone ask for fresh dvisti?" he calls out, grinning in my direction.

"That's definitely fresh," I admit, since he seems to be looking at me for a response. What, does he want a pat on the back for hunting? I offer him a faint smile. "Thank you, I think?"

"The chief said I should bring this here to your cave." He tosses the enormous, dead thing down onto the floor with a *whump*. "So you can have fresh meat and skins."

Josie looks at me, and I can see panic on her face. I'm feeling a hint of panic, too. We've helped out with chores before, but this is the first time we've had to process a kill on our own from start to finish. "You shouldn't have," I say, putting the belt I'm weaving aside and getting to my feet. "Really."

Cashol is undeterred by my tepid response. "You do not look happy. Is this not a fine kill? Look at these flanks." He slaps the thing's backside. "So much meat. This will keep you busy for days, yes?"

Josie looks like she's ready to cry. She picks up a skinning knife and then stares at it, and I know how she feels. That small knife made entirely of bone and rock seems wholly inadequate for the task at hand...yet the sa-khui do it all the time, without complaint. It can be done. It just feels like a lot.

I feel a bubble of panic rising in my chest and shove a lock of hair behind my ear. "Um...." I wring my hands thinking. "Thank...you?"

As if Cashol can sense my hesitation, his blowhard expression softens and he glances at Josie, then at me. He gets to his feet, one of those goofy smiles curving his mouth as he leans in toward me. "May I ask a favor?"

Oh god, what now? There's more? Is he going to dump this dead animal's friend on our doorstep, too? But politeness makes me answer. "Sure?"

"Will you females allow me to show off my prowess for a bit?" He pulls a knife from his belt and postures, and I get a mental image of dudes flexing to impress the ladies, barbarian style. "I would love to show you my skills at skinning and processing a kill."

And he flexes again.

A surge of relief courses through me at the understanding look in Cashol's warm eyes. He knows we're intimidated and he's being a dork deliberately to make us smile. And he's going to help out. I'm filled with such a rush of gratitude that my heart flutters in my chest. I smile warmly at him.

Then, my heart flutters again.

It jumps in my chest so hard that I immediately go still, clutching at my chest. What the—

It does it again, and then I hear it. Purring. Not gentle or sweet or hesitant, but loud and violent and demanding. My cootie is awake, and it's resonating.

I push my hand into my tunic, press my palm against my skin. There's no mistaking it—my cootie is on fire. And when I look up, Cashol is staring at me with a dazed expression, his hand on his chest, too.

So.

This is my mate.

I'm stunned with the realization. This alien man right here

is my partner, my mate, my forever. I'm both relieved and utterly terrified.

This is what I wanted, right? This is my safety net. This is my ticket to getting to stay with the tribe forever.

So...why am I so terrified?

I hide my terror, though. I let out a squeal of giddiness and fling myself into Cashol's arms, feigning happiness. In a way, I am happy. I am. "It's you," I say to him, beaming, and I try not to think about the worry and terror worming its way through my system.

I thought so much about resonance, and how much I hoped for it.

I just never stopped to think about what happened *after*.

And now I'm going to have to deal with a whole lot of after. But I press a kiss to Cashol's mouth and squeal as if I'm the most delighted woman ever.

5

CASHOL

This is the greatest day of my existence. I have resonated to the female I would have chosen for myself, the one that makes my heart sing, the one that makes me smile every time I see her. It is as if my khui has heard the demands of my heart and decided that it would please me with its choice.

Truly, the ancestors' spirits have smiled down upon us this day. I beam with pride as my tribesmates approach and clap us both on the back. Meh-gan has a bewildered expression on her face, but it is understandable. Her little friend—the noisy one—shrieks and jumps and makes so much noise that I start to think perhaps Haeden is right, that she is far too loud. But then my chief is there, and the elders, and everyone is so happy for us. Meh-gan clutches at my arm, her khui singing loudly to mine, and I want nothing more than to escape all the madness and attention and drag her into the furs.

It is difficult to listen when an elder is congratulating me on my mate when my cock is hard and straining for that mate under my loincloth. My body's reaction to resonance was immediate, and it is growing increasingly tricky to ignore. I want nothing more than to toss Meh-gan down onto the furs and plow into her soft body. I need to relieve the ache in my groin and the hungry need that pumps through my veins. More than anything, there is an all-consuming desire to claim her, to please her, and it is...distracting.

Not that my tribe has noticed. They are too busy congratulating us and planning a celebration.

Vektal knows how I feel, though. He sees the strain on my face behind my smile and gestures at one of the supply caves. "Before we celebrate anything, let us give them a home and privacy. You need your own cave."

"Thank you, my chief," I tell him, relieved.

Meh-gan just holds my arm tighter, that bright smile on her face.

The storage cave is cleared out with the helping hands of many, enough left for a bed of furs for myself and my new mate, and a few items to start our own cave. We will fill it with comforts later, but for now, all we need is a bed and a fire. Drenol makes the fire for us, and pats my arm as he walks back to the elders' cave. A privacy screen is produced, a plate of food and a flask of sah-sah shoved into my arms, and then Meh-gan and I are left alone in our new cave.

She stares at me.

I stare at her, grinning. The only sound between us is the intense singing of our khuis to one another. She has said nothing beyond a few happy squeals earlier, and I worry she is starting to panic. The smile on her face looks...brittle, like thin ice.

She looks tired.

More than that, she looks slightly terrified.

"Well," I say after a long moment. "This day has not turned out as planned."

Her mouth twitches, just a little. "That's an understatement." Meh-gan glances around the cave. She looks so uncertain. It is a wildly different reaction than the Meh-gan that squealed and pressed her mouth to mine in one of the mouth-matings the humans are so fond of.

Mouth-matings. My body aches just thinking about that, and my cock feels as if it is made of stone. But I remember what Vektal said about Meh-gan, and how she is healing still. Her body might be fine but her heart is not. That much is clear.

So even if I want to fling her down into the furs, I must go slow. Resonance changes nothing except it has made my body hungry for hers, my cock aching without relief. My body—my pleasure—will just have to wait.

I turn away, discreetly adjusting myself and pretending to look around the cave. "Does this place please you, Meh-gan? If you do not like it, I can ask Vektal for a different cave—"

"No, it's fine!" Her words are rushed, and when I turn to look at her, she offers another hesitant smile. "It's the best. Please tell him thank you."

I grin at her. "You can thank him, as well."

She makes a noise in her throat that might be agreement, and her gaze falls to the bed. "Um, should we..."

"I would like to talk first," I lie, and make a mental note to adjust myself once more.

"Talk?" Her bewildered expression flashes with relief. "Of course we can talk. That's fine."

I sit down, cross-legged, and she sits down next to me. That is both good and bad. Good, because I like her nearness. Bad, because I like her nearness too much. I busy myself taking off my boots, unwrapping the laces and getting comfortable. I do not think we will be leaving this cave for a while, so I might as well relax.

She watches me in silence, saying nothing. I glance over, and when I toss my second boot aside, her cheeks seem to be pink in a flush. "Is this all right?" I ask, gesturing at my now-bare feet. "You will tell me if I offend you in some way? I do not know human customs."

"You're fine. It's all fine." Her cheeks grow pinker. "You, um, have big feet."

"Yes," I agree, wiggling my toes. "I have tripped over them many a time, too."

Meh-gan chuckles, and the sound ripples over me like warm water, pleasant and smooth....and settles right in my groin.

Slow, I remind myself. Slow.

I casually grab a fur and toss it over my lap, pretending to shiver. "Cold?"

She shrugs, staring at the fire.

I pick up another blanket and put it on her shoulders, feeling very, very obvious. Outside the cave, music begins. It is a slow drum beat, signaling the beginning of a celebration. There will be feasting, and much drinking of fermented sah-sah. Farli will insist everyone get painted with symbols and all will have a good time, celebrating the mating they think I am doing with Meh-gan. They will celebrate another mating, and a kit to be born.

A kit.

The thought hits me and I feel flattened at the realization that I will be a father. I have concentrated on the pleasant aspects of resonance only—the mating, the bond between myself and Meh-gan, the mating...more mating...but after we come together and resonance is satisfied, there will be a kit. I will be a father.

I swallow hard. I am not certain I am ready to be a father. I think of my own father, who died when I was young, when the khui sickness leveled half the tribe. I remember as he lay in his sickbed, he rambled to me while I held his hand. He spoke of my mother in long stretches, which was surprising to me because he'd never spoken of her. He spoke of how resonance had been the greatest thing that had ever happened to him, and the worst. He had loved my mother greatly and had been beyond joy to resonate to her...only to lose her in childbirth when I was born.

I have always remembered that. Resonance can be incredible...and it can also be the greatest of tragedies.

I look over at Meh-gan, and I decide that going slow is wise. I want to go as slow as I can to draw this out. I am not ready to be a father.

I am not ready to lose her. My throat constricts at the thought.

I must stall. I must find some way to slow down resonance.

"Will you tell me about yourself, Meh-gan?" I ask, lounging backward. "Let us learn about one another."

She stares at my feet for a moment longer, then tears her gaze away. "W-what?"

"Let us learn about one another."

"Oh. Um." She tucks a strand of yellow mane behind one ridiculously small pink ear. "Like...what?"

"Do you...like hunting?"

Meh-gan looks at me as if I have grown another head. "No."

"Have you tried it?" I have not seen her leave the caves. "Perhaps you might."

She shrugs, that mystified look still on her face.

Her shoulders move in a way that makes my cock twitch. Resonance is...potent. I take a calming breath and try to think of something else to ask her. Can I bury my face between your thighs? Can I touch you? Can I make you cry out with pleasure? All of those things float to the top of my head, but I discard them one by one. I must ask her small things. Simple things. "Do you...like leather?"

Meh-gan blinks at me. "I...guess? It beats being naked. Why are you asking me this?"

I am making a fool of myself. I stare at my bare feet, thinking. "I just wish to get to know you. That is all."

"By asking me if I like leather? That's like asking if I enjoy breathing air. Leather's kinda necessary here, isn't it?"

"Yes, but it is new to your people, is it not? That is why I asked. You wore other things when you were home?"

She nods, her expression relaxing a bit. "I wouldn't say leather is new to us, just that we've moved beyond it. We grow plants called 'cotton' and they have little puffballs on them, and you take the puffs and weave them into fabric. It's kinda a long process."

I try to picture this, and snicker.

"What's so funny?"

"I do not see why wearing a tunic made of puffballs is better than leather."

Her pink mouth twitches, and I am enchanted at the sight. "It's not a cloak of puffballs. It makes like...flat fabric. I don't know. All I know is I used to walk into the store and buy a shirt without having to think about where it came from, and now if I want clothes, I have to kill an animal and take its skin. It's a big adjustment." She shifts uncomfortably. "But I'm sure I'll get used to it and be making all kinds of clothes in no time."

"If you like." I have no worries that she will find her way to be useful. Everyone does. When she falls silent again, I prompt her. "Do you wish to ask me a question?"

She twists her hands in her lap, then shrugs. "How old are you?"

"By our seasons? I have seen twenty-six of them. You?"

"I don't know how old I am by your seasons." Meh-gan's mouth curves into a smile. "But I'm twenty-two by human years. So you're not that much older than me, huh?"

"Not at all." I roll onto my side, facing her. I like the little smile that plays around her lips. "Do you want me to be older? I can pretend."

She snorts. "Just be you."

"Very well." I consider this for a moment. "What is your favorite meal?"

I could swear Meh-gan rolls her eyes at me ever so slightly. "Are you being serious right now?"

"Why would I not be serious?"

She gestures at our surroundings. "We resonated. And you're asking me about my favorite meal?" Her gaze focuses on me and her expression grows a little anxious. "Do you...do you not like me? I thought...never mind. It isn't important."

I am going about this all wrong, I realize, when she starts to get up. I grab her hand before she can, and she pauses, watching me. She is skittish like a dvisti colt, ready to bolt, and I think Vektal was wise indeed to advise me to take things slow. "It is not like that at all. I like you very much. Of all the human females, I would have picked you for a mate."

"*Just* humans?"

"Out of all females," I amend, amused at her prickly nature. I prefer this to her frozen smile. "I have never been interested in Maylak or Asha and the other two have been mated for as long as I can remember."

"Then why aren't we, you know..." She gestures at the furs. "Doing it? I thought that's what happened the moment you resonated. And I feel, well..." Meh-gan flushes again. "I definitely feel like my body is ready."

"Your body may be ready," I concede, "But...I am not sure I am."

Her brows furrow. "What, are you shy?"

It is the perfect answer. I jump on it. "Yes. I am very shy."

"You?"

"I have never had a mate of any sort." This is very much the truth, though it does not make me shy. Hungry and near-feral with need, yes, but not shy. However, if Meh-gan thinks I am shy, then she will not be hurt when I suggest we take things slow. It is the perfect solution. "This is all very new to me and I would get to know you before we leap into the furs."

Meh-gan stares at me with clear surprise. She thinks for a moment, then bites her lip. "I'm sorry. I guess I just assumed since you were flirting with me that you were experienced. You know what they say about assuming, though."

"No, what do they say?" I tilt my head, curious.

"It doesn't matter." She reaches out and takes my hand, and just the brush of her small, soft fingers against my callused hands is enough to make my cock twitch. Hot need courses through me, and she says something in a soft, gentle voice, but I do not hear it. The blood is pounding too hard in my ears. I cannot come. I cannot come.

Not yet. Not when parts of me are supposed to be shy. Those parts are not paying attention, though, as my cock is still rock hard.

She lets go of my hand, and it is easier to concentrate. Her lips move, and eventually the roaring in my ears dies down.

I smile. This will be easy. So easy. I will take things slow and I will know when Meh-gan is ready when her smile reaches her eyes.

6

CASHOL

Meh-gan and I lie in the furs in silence, listening to the chatter in the main cave and the endless beat of the drum. The celebration sounds like a good one, and delicious smells waft through, teasing our noses in our "private" cave. I should not be thinking about food. I should be claiming my mate in every way possible, but since I am not, I wonder what they are eating. I wonder if there will be extra left over for me for when I go out to hunt tomorrow.

Then I wonder if I am even going to hunt tomorrow. It might be impossible to do with my aching, still-hard cock erect between my thighs.

Meh-gan lies on her back, staring up at the ceiling. Her fingers drum on her abdomen, and she seems lost in thought. I watch her for a moment, enjoying the sight of the small, rounded tip of her nose and the point of her chin. She glances over at me, and then blushes when she catches me staring.

"What is it?" I ask.

"Do you think everyone thinks we're making out?"

'Making out'? I do not know what this means, but I can guess. "I am positive that they think we are mating feverishly, yes."

Her cheeks grow pinker. "How long do you think we can hold out? Before it affects us?"

Before it affects us? I am already feeling affected. It feels as if I have no blood left in the top half of my body. I adjust myself again under the blankets, thinking. How long has anyone ever lasted before giving in? Most do not even bother to fight. There was Zalah and Haeden, but that did not end well and I try not to think about it. "I do not know."

"We're probably not going to be able to take it that slow, then."

I cannot tell if this makes her happy or not. "True, but it does not have to happen tonight. We can relax for a bit." I reach out and cautiously put my hand on hers, wondering how she will react to that small touch.

She squeezes my fingers, and my cock near spills in my loincloth. "You're a good man, Cashol."

"You have not spent much time talking to Haeden if you think that," I tease.

Meh-gan chuckles, glancing over at me, and I am filled with such hot yearning at the sight of her face that I lose my breath. She watches me, her expression uncertain. Her gaze dips to my mouth, and I remember how she pressed her lips there. A mouth-mating, Vektal has called it. Humans like to do that, to press their tongues inside the mouth of their partners. I received no tongue...and I decide I am sad about it.

"What are you thinking about?" she asks suddenly.

"I am thinking about when you put your mouth on mine earlier. Vektal has told us that Shorshie uses tongue and I have not yet decided if I should tell him that she did it wrong."

Meh-gan rolls onto her side, propping her head up on one

hand. "How do you know Georgie's the one that did it wrong? Maybe I did."

"Impossible. You can do nothing wrong."

She snorts.

"Besides, it felt really good," I tell her. "I am not sure that adding tongue would improve upon it."

"Oh, it does."

"It does?" I sit up. "Are you sure?"

"I've done it lots of times." Meh-gan hesitates, then sits up as well. "Cashol, you should know that I'm not a virgin. I've had sex."

I stare at her, the blood pounding through my veins once more. Never have I heard anything better than the sound of my name on her lips.

"You could say something, you know," she whispers.

"Say it again," I tell her. "My name."

"Cashol?" She is soft and breathless this time.

I groan, closing my eyes, and my hand goes to the front of my pants. I clench my cock in my grip, trying to control myself. I want to hear her say it over and over again, but I know I will not last if she does.

"I'm trying to tell you that I'm not a virgin—"

"It does not matter," I manage to choke out.

"But you waited for a mate—"

I laugh. "Only because there were no options. My hand received quite a lot of attention, though."

Her eyes widen, and she giggles. Relief crosses her face. "You...you don't care?"

"No, why would I?" I do not like the thought of another male touching her—not at all. She is mine. But humans are very different. How can I blame her for something she did in another life? "All that matters is here and now."

"No, that's not all that matters." Her mouth presses into a

firm line and she rubs a hand over her brow. "I...have something else to tell you."

"Do you promise to say it like you did my name?"

Her mouth twitches. "Are you ever serious?"

"Sometimes. Not when it means I can make you smile instead."

"I'm trying to tell you something important." She gives my shoulder a nudge. "Something that might make you look at me differently."

"Then say it and let me be the judge." I suspect I already know.

Her hands fall to her lap and twist in the blankets. "I was pregnant when I got kidnapped. And...I was going to keep it."

"Of course you were going to keep it." I am confused.

"No, I mean, I was going to have someone else's baby." Her eyes fill with tears. "It was just some guy I met at a club. A meaningless fling. I didn't expect it to be anything, but then I found out I was pregnant and everything changed." Her chin drops and she stares at her hands. "And then they took it from me."

I hate her sadness. I want to say a million silly things so she will look at me and roll her eyes. I want her to not be sad. I want her to smile. I do not know how to do any of these things, though, but I remember how my father used to hug me when I was a kit, and how Sevvah hugged me when I lost him. She was my parent when I had none, and I could always go to her for a warm embrace. So I give that to Meh-gan now. I pull her in my arms and stroke her mane, just like how Sevvah did to me when I was sad. "How can I make it better for you?"

Something inside her breaks. A muffled little sob escapes her and she clings to my vest, holding tight to me as she weeps. I tuck her under my chin and rub her back, wanting more than anything for her to stop crying. For her sadness to leave her. I cannot fix it for her, but I can at least hold her. So I do.

Eventually, her sniffles subside and she swipes at her face. "You're really nice, you know." She sniffs again. "My cootie made a good pick."

"I think there are several males in this tribe that would argue that point."

"It doesn't matter what they think," she tells me earnestly, sitting up and meeting my eyes. "You are the nicest, kindest alien I have ever met and I feel really lucky that if I had to resonate, it was to you." Her gaze flicks to my mouth again for a moment, and I wonder if she is thinking about when she pressed hers to mine.

I have to ask. I cannot help myself. My cock is too heavy with seed to let the issue slide. "When you put your mouth on mine earlier...why did you do it?"

She raises her shoulders ever so slightly. "It was a kiss. Humans do it when we're happy with a partner or in love."

"Then why did you do it to me?"

"Because it's expected. We're mates."

This does not fill me with confidence. "Is that why you did not give me tongue?"

Meh-gan lets out a horrified giggle. "What? No, I just...it's impolite to start tonguing someone in front of a bunch of people."

"Not to me," I tease. "I would welcome such a greeting."

She chuckles again, and I can see her mood lightening. "I'll keep that in mind for the future."

I like the thought of a future with her. I keep my arms around her, because she feels good in my arms. She fits there perfectly. "So then, may I ask you more questions?"

"It depends. Are you going to ask me about more leather?" She arches one pale brow at me.

"I promise I shall not." I rub a hand up and down her back, and I notice she does not pull away from me as I do. "Will you tell me what you like in a mate?"

"What I like?"

"Yes."

She wears a puzzled expression. "Why does it matter? We resonated."

She does not understand that I am trying to go slow. That I am trying to find things about me that she might like, so that I can entice her into looking at resonance as a good thing, instead of the resigned look on her face. "What is your favorite body part?"

Meh-gan sputters, laughing. "My favorite body part?"

"I am serious," I tell her, but I smile, too. "I wish to know. What is it that my pretty Meh-gan finds appealing?"

Her expression softens. "Do you find me pretty? Even though I'm not sa-khui?"

"Very much so. And I do not say that simply because I resonate."

She chuckles. "What's your favorite part, then?"

I consider this. "Perhaps your ears."

"My ears?"

"They are so tiny." I reach out to touch one with a fingertip. "And they go pink when you are embarrassed."

Meh-gan giggles, ducking her head when I touch her earlobe. "I'm ticklish."

"And now I am wanting to touch them more," I admit. The realization that she is ticklish just makes my cock harder. But I drop my hand, because I must go slow, even if it is torture.

"If it helps," she offers after a minute, her cheeks charmingly pink, "I like your feet."

I glance down. "My...feet?" They are big, sure, but they seem normal to me. They are just...feet. "You like them?"

Her face grows even pinker. "I just...like feet. And you have nice ones."

"You can touch them if you like." I wonder if it is possible for me to come just from her hand on my feet. Probably.

But Meh-gan only ducks her head, burying it against my shoulder. "Not yet."

"Of course not. Can I see your feet?"

I notice that her breath speeds up and I suspect that Meh-gan's ears are not the only thing that is sensitive and ticklish. She hesitates for a moment, and then nods, scooting away from me on the furs. I expect her to undo her boots herself, but she lifts one foot and holds it in the air, indicating that I should take care of it.

I grin. She is bossy. I like this. I much prefer a demanding mate to a terrified one.

7

CASHOL

I take her small foot in my lap and carefully unwrap her boot, removing the leather laces and unwinding them with great care, then tugging her foot free. Her toes wriggle the moment they are exposed to air, and I laugh at the sight of them. "Look at how tiny this extra toe is."

"It's not extra!"

"It is! What do you need that for? There is no point to it." I wiggle my toes, comparing to her five small ones. "I can almost understand why you have an extra finger, but all those extra toes? It is just wasteful. All you need is three strong ones."

"Oh please. My feet aren't weird. Yours are weird with only three toes."

"You just told me you liked them, though. Does that mean you like weird?" I touch her tiny fifth toe, fascinated by the fat, stubby length of it. Just a pink little blob, that toe. It is adorable. When she doesn't answer me, I take her other foot into my hands and strip her other boot off. "So many toes," I joke. "I could bite them off and then we would be even." I lean down and mockingly pretend as if I am going to take a bite out of her foot.

Meh-gan sucks in a breath.

I hesitate for just a moment, because the look on her face has gone from laughing to intense. Her pupils look huge in the blue sea of her eyes, and her khui seems louder than ever. Fascinated, I pull her foot to my mouth and suck on one of her small toes. I capture it in my mouth and run my tongue over it, watching her reaction.

Meh-gan moans, a little shudder moving over her body.

I groan, lowering her foot. Now I am the one that is panting, because her reaction is not a reaction I should encourage. Her feet are sensitive, and here I am licking them after I promised my chief I would go slow. This is not slow.

This is a mistake, and yet I immediately want to lick her again.

The scent of her arousal hangs in the air, rich and thick, and I groan, leaning back against the cave wall and closing my eyes. "I should not have done that."

"W-why not?" Meh-gan's voice is husky, soft. "I liked it."

Her khui is so loud that it is distracting me. So is her scent. I want nothing more than to grab her and bury my face between her thighs. "I wanted to go slow," I grit out. "That was not very slow of me."

"Oh." She gently pulls her foot out of my grip, and I reluctantly let her go. I expect her to move away, but instead, she sits on her knees, moving closer to me. She shifts her weight, then reaches up and tucks a lock of my mane behind my ear, her fingers grazing the curve of my ear and then touching my earlobe. "Why do you want to go so slow? Are you nervous?"

What can I possibly tell her? I nod, swallowing hard. This part is true; I am a little nervous, but mostly because I wish to make it good for her. I do not want her thinking about all that she has lost, or having regrets that she has mated to silly, foolish Cashol who is not nearly as handsome as his cousin Vektal or as clever with a spear as his friend Haeden. "Nervous. Yes."

"I understand," she whispers, and slides her arm around my shoulders. Our faces are but a handspan apart, and she studies me, her gaze flicking to my mouth before she looks me in the eye once more. "We don't have to move too fast, but I liked it when you touched me."

I close my eyes, breathing hard, because I am in danger of spilling my seed all over my leathers. "I liked touching you, too. Far too much."

Meh-gan chuckles. "I don't think there's such a thing." Her hand goes to my chest, and she strokes her fingers over my collarbone, pausing at the plating over my heart. "Your skin is so soft. I've never felt anything like it."

It is as if her hand is directly on my cock, it feels so good. I groan again, my hand flexing at my side as I try desperately not to grab at her. "I am...glad...you like it," I manage to choke out. "I wore....my favorite skin....for you."

She giggles, then leans in and brushes her lips over my jaw. "You're so weird sometimes."

I let out a hard breath, gazing at her as she moves ever closer. Her hand rests on my chest, her arm around my shoulders, and I can feel her breath on my skin, warm and sweet. Her teats push up against my chest as she moves even closer, and then she leans in, her lips a whisper away from mine.

"Want to try kissing again?"

As if I could ever refuse such a request. "I would." I cannot stop staring at her lovely, pink mouth. At her soft lips, her inviting smile. Truly, of all the humans, she is the prettiest. How did she end up with me? "Or I can just lick your feet again," I offer. "Whatever you like."

Meh-gan just smiles, all confidence, and puts a finger on my chin. She turns my face toward hers, and then brushes her mouth to mine.

I let out a shuddering breath. It is the briefest of kisses, scarcely more than a nudge. "Am I greedy if I say I hoped that would last longer?"

Her smile widens. "It's called a warm-up. We'll do more."

"I am definitely warm."

She presses her lips to mine again, this time more than just a nudge. This time, she nips at my lower lip, then kisses my upper one. She peppers my mouth with more soft, gentle kisses, and I remain completely still, not wanting to break the spell of this. It is the most perfect thing I have ever experienced.

She is the most perfect thing.

Meh-gan's lashes flutter, and then she slants her mouth fully over mine. Her lips are parted, and her tongue teases out against the seam of my mouth.

I cannot stop the groan that escapes me. I clench her against my chest, pulling her back to me when she pulls away. "More," I demand, and love when she chuckles and complies. Her arms twine around my neck even as she puts her lips on mine again. Then, her tongue strokes ever so softly into my mouth. It is smooth and warm, her tongue, and it is as if she is licking my cock when she licks at my mouth.

I hiss and drop a hand to my cock, pressing hard against it so I do not spill.

"Feels good?" Meh-gan whispers, a question on her face. She tilts her head, watching me, then leans in and kisses me again, her tongue playing against mine even as her hand slides low. She covers my hand—where I still grip my cock—and then gently nudges my hand aside.

Her fingers stroke me through my leather, outlining my length and teasing the sides of my shaft.

I groan against her mouth, even as the kiss takes on a hungrier pace. I try to remember all the things my cousin said about kissing his mate, about what she liked, but all I can think about is Meh-gan's flirty little tongue flicking against mine, Meh-gan's hand rubbing up and down my length, Meh-gan's teats pressing against my chest—

I cannot contain myself. The release bubbles up through me, and I grab her hand and drag it roughly up and down my cock, working myself to a quick, hard release. I shudder as I come, my seed boiling over, and truly, I am surprised I lasted as long as I did.

So much for slow.

Meh-gan nips at my lower lip again, then slides her tongue over the place she bit. "That was...fast."

"Embarrassingly so."

Her smile widens. "No need to be embarrassed. You said this is your first time. As long as you feel good, it doesn't matter." Her hand strokes up and down my twitching length, now sticky underneath my leathers. "Do you want to clean up? We can talk more if you like." She's breathless and soft like this, her expression achingly sweet.

I do not like what she is suggesting, though. Clean up and talk? Not when she has not yet experienced the same pleasure. "I want to make you come first." I lean in, rubbing my nose against hers as I try to capture her mouth in a kiss. "Can I touch you?"

"Where?"

Slow, I chant to myself. Slow. Slow. I want to bury my face between her thighs, but that is not slow. "Your...feet?"

She takes my hand and guides it to her waistband. "You can touch me here, instead."

"Your stomach?" I tease, but I am breathless and foolish and trying to make a joke even when I want nothing more than to touch her there.

Meh-gan shakes her head and guides my hand lower, into

her leggings. "But you have to kiss me," she whispers, lifting her mouth to mine. "Please."

"Do you want me?" I have to ask, because I am dying to hear her say such things.

She hesitates, then brushes her lips against mine. "I want release, Cashol. Please."

It should be enough. She is being honest. We are still strangers to each other. Even so, I am oddly hurt. I hide this with a cocky grin, and press my mouth to hers. "Say my name again," I demand. If I cannot have a declaration of lust from her, I will take my name whispered on her lips.

"Cashol," she says, and whimpers when my fingers stroke over the mound of curls between her thighs.

Touching her is fascinating, and I forget all about any fleeting hurt I might have felt. This is my mate under my hand, I realize with awe. My mate whose khui is thrumming a sharp, needy song in her chest as I caress her. My mate, who has strange curls between her thighs, and a slit that is so, so wet that it makes my cock stir all over again.

I mate my mouth with hers, ravenous for more of Meh-gan, of her soft sighs and the way she clings to me as my fingers explore up and down her sweet cunt. She squirms against my hand, as if trying to silently nudge me one way or another. I kiss her again, and then murmur, "Where do you want my fingers, Meh-gan? Show me where on your cunt."

She whimpers, biting at my lower lip even as she guides my hand. She steers me with a touch, and when my stroking fingers brush over a small nub hidden at the apex of her cunt, she gasps. Aha. I remember Vektal telling us of a third nipple. This must be it. Hungrily, I stare down at her covered teats, wondering what it would be like to touch them as I brush my fingers over that spot again.

"Small...circles..." she pants, grabbing my jaw and kissing me again. "Circles."

I grin. "You are very bossy—"

"Shush," she tells me, and moans again, her fingers curling against the protective plating on my arms when I hit the right spot. "Oh fuck, just like that."

My smile turns into a groan as she grows slicker around my fingers. Her legs twitch, opening wider for my hand, and I devour her mouth, stroking my tongue against hers. "Meh-gan," I demand, my hunger for her ramping up again already. "Say my name as I touch you." My other hand moves to her silky, pale mane, and I grab a handful of it as she practically crawls into my lap with her need. "Say it."

"Cashol," she gasps, her mouth hungry for mine. "Oh, keep doing that, Cashol."

"I will not stop," I promise her, and even if my hand should fall off, I will keep touching her, just like this. I watch her, entranced, as she bucks against my hand, my fingers so wet her cunt is slippery against my skin, and every time her flesh meets mine, it makes a slick sound that hardens my cock. "Ride my hand," I tell her, then bite at her neck. "Ride me. Use me."

She moans, her hips jerking against my hand. There is a fresh round of wetness and her entire body quivers against me. She goes stiff, gasping, and then sags against me, boneless. Meh-gan buries her face against my neck and I hold her close, stroking her mane as she comes to herself again.

"Thank you," she eventually whispers to me.

I fight back a frown. Why is she thanking me? I am her mate. It is my duty to ensure that she receives pleasure when we touch. This is not a chore for me. This is a great joy...but she acts as if she is asking for favors. I do not understand it. I slide my fingers over her cunt again, because my cock is hard and I am ready to touch her more, but she makes a noise of distress. I remove my hand and kiss her smooth brow instead. "Next time, I want to use my mouth instead of my hand."

She chuckles. "Next time, I'll let you."

I try to pull her close, to hold her against me as we relax, but she slides out of my grasp and retreats to the far side of the blankets.

"Would you like a drink?" I ask her. "Or are you hungry?"

"I'm okay," Meh-gan tells me with a faint smile. I sense that she is lost in her thoughts. Even though we are here together, in our cave, it feels as if I am alone.

I am a foolish hunter to be hurt over such things. I rub my chest, listening to the frantic song of my unsatisfied khui, and try not to worry. This is all new for Meh-gan. I am to go slow. I am to give her time. She must come to terms with her sadness before she can embrace another with joy.

But oh, it is hard, to want her adoration and receive only polite smiles instead. I get to my feet, wincing at the squish of my leathers as I move. I get a bowl of water and use tongs to put a hot rock from the fire into it, then turn my back to her and clean my cock off, switching to a fresh loincloth. She says nothing as I change clothes, and I feel even more alone.

I remind myself that she kissed me.

I remind myself that she reached for my cock. I did not force her. She wanted me.

It must be enough for now. I take the bowl of warm water and sit down next to her on the furs. "May I wash you, my mate?"

"I can do it," she says quickly, and takes the bowl from me.

Even this small pleasure, I am denied. I bite back a sigh.

Slow. I must move slow.

8

MEGAN

My new cave—the one I'm going to share with Cashol for the rest of my life—feels entirely too small. I stare up at the ceiling, unable to sleep, and constantly, permanently aware of Cashol at my side. His big presence is everywhere, and there's no corner I can escape to without being confronted with him, his gorgeous, lanky body, his easygoing grin, the penetrating look in his eyes. The sound of his cootie, constantly revving like a motorboat.

He gives me such hot, searing looks every time we make eye contact that I wonder at his shyness at all. He doesn't seem shy. Incredibly eager, yes. Shy? Not so much. I suspect the "shyness" is an excuse for his stamina, which probably won't be much since he's a virgin. And that's fine with me. I'm certainly not going to hold it against him. Things like that come with time and practice, and since we're both still resonating like crazy, I imagine he'll get time *and* experience in spades.

I shift uncomfortably on the blankets. He made me come

earlier, but my body still feels...well, revved up. Like I've been ignoring my needs for a thousand years and it's all coming to crash down on me at once. My skin feels hot and achy, and I'm twitchy, and I want nothing more than to grab his hand and shove it between my legs again.

This resonance thing is potent.

As if my cootie can hear my dirty thoughts, it revs even louder, which is terribly awkward in the small cave. I try to ignore it, hugging the blankets higher on my chest, studying the ceiling with great enthusiasm as Cashol looks over at me again.

"You cannot sleep?"

I shrug, then take the coward's way out and blame it on the party still going just outside our doorstep. "Hard to with that going on. Aren't they tired?"

He chuckles. "It seems not." He reaches over and very carefully brushes a lock of hair off my forehead, as if he can't bear to not touch me.

It's...sweet. It's nice. It also makes my nipples harden so desperately that it feels like I've got two lighthouse beacons sticking out of the front of my tunic, flashing for attention. I glance over at him and he's watching me with another hungry look on his face that makes my entire body flush with awareness. I can't bring myself to make the first move, though. I feel like this needs to be his choice.

If I fling myself at him, I'm always going to worry that he didn't want this nearly as much as I do. That I'm forcing myself upon him just to ensure I have a home here. I doubt he's thinking that—Cashol is nice, above all else—but I can't help but feel that way. It feels like I'm trading sex for security, which is the same situation the alien kidnappers had me in.

I hate that I'm thinking like that—no matter how true it is—so I pick at the blankets and offer him a faint smile. "Are you not sleepy, either?"

He shakes his head. "My mind is too full of noise."

"The party noise?"

Cashol reaches out and traces his finger along my hairline. For a moment, I think he's smoothing my hair back again, but when he continues, I realize he's just using this as an excuse to touch me. His fingertips move at the edge of my brow, and I swear, it feels like the most erotic touch ever. "Other noise. Noise in my thoughts."

I know just what he means. My brain won't shut down, either.

"Would you like to go hunting with me tomorrow?" Cashol asks, his fingertip gliding over one of my brows. "I am not sure if it is resonance or something else, but I do not like the thought of being apart from you, even for an afternoon."

The thought of him leaving makes me feel curiously panicky, too. He's my safety net, my lifeline in this crazy world. I don't want him going anywhere. I grab his hand and hold it to my chest, just over my heart—and my singing cootie. "You're leaving?"

"I would not go far," he promises. The heated look in his eyes deepens as he gazes down at our joined hands. "Just a small hunt. It is my duty as a hunter to provide for the tribe."

"But you just resonated. Is there a rule that says you have to go back out right away?"

"No."

I rub my thumb over his knuckles, and lord, do my breasts ache. All of me aches, but I want to grab his hand, shove it under my leather tunic, and just drag it to all my sensitive spots. I lick my lips, feeling ever so slightly breathless, and try to remain casual. "Are you even going to be able to walk tomorrow?" If he feels anything like I do, the answer will be a firm "no." I don't think I can even cross the room without getting weak in the knees. I can't imagine leaving the cave to try and do something productive like hunting.

He gives me a sheepish smile. "Perhaps not. Very well, then. My invitation to go hunting together will stand for the next time I go out, then. When I am able to walk without being in pain."

That makes me freeze. "You're in pain?"

Cashol gives me a faint grimace. "More like a constant ache?"

Oh. Of course. I glance down his chest, my gaze on his loincloth. He's wearing nothing else, and I can see his enormous, beautiful feet peeking out from underneath his furs. He's not sharing furs with me, which is probably for the best. I think. "Are you sure you want to go slow, then?"

"Absolutely," he manages, but his voice is hoarse.

I'm pretty sure he's lying. My cootie purrs a bit louder, and something clenches deep inside me. What is he stalling for? What is the problem here?

Is it...me?

Does he need a nudge? I told myself I was going to let this be all his idea, but maybe this odd shyness is getting in his way. I lift our joined hands to my lips and gently brush his knuckles with a kiss. "I'm sorry you're hurting."

He groans, his gaze rapt on me.

"Has anything gone down?"

"Gone...down?"

I point at the blankets. "Downstairs?"

"Down...stairs?"

Right. They don't have stairs here. He's not going to get my euphemisms. "Is your cock bothering you?"

That makes his crooked, silly smile return. "I would not say it is *bothering* me." He pauses. "But it is rather alert."

I chuckle. This man is so very strange, yet endearing. "Can I ask you something?"

"Anything."

I nip at his knuckles, and I swear his eyes darken with lust.

It makes me feel powerful to do that, and I know I'm flirting with danger, with pushing him just a touch too far, but I can't seem to help myself. "What about this makes you shy? Is it me?"

His throat bobs, Adam's apple working. "It is...complicated."

"You can tell me." Lord, if anyone understands complicated feelings, it's certainly me. "I won't judge you."

"I just..." He sits up. Rubs his hand over his mouth. I notice he keeps the other one locked in my grasp, as if he's unwilling to let go of me for a moment. Cashol stares at the wall, and I wait for his answer, curious. "I feel we should take things slow."

"Is it because you had feelings for someone else?"

He glances over at me, that crooked smile beaming. "Never. I have only seen you, even when you did not know my name."

Ooh, ouch. I feel a bit like a jerk. "Are you worried I won't like it? Or that you won't have enough stamina? Because if it's not perfect, that's fine." I nip at his knuckles again, then rest our joined hands against my breastbone, letting his hand brush against my bare skin where my collar is open. "I don't expect perfect."

He's panting, unable to look away from me. Is that a hint of sweat on his brow? For a man that wants to go slow, he sure gets worked up easily. "I just..."

"Yes?"

"Want..."

I wait.

"To...go slow," he manages to strangle out.

9

MEGAN

I blink.

I'm getting nowhere with him. A new idea occurs to me. "Are you waiting for me to make the first move?"

He scoffs. "Of course not." But his gaze lands on our joined hands, and I can feel his tail twitching. There's such aching need in his gaze that it's baffling. It's clear he wants me. It's also clear that he's stalling for some reason...and he won't tell me what it is.

"Do you not want to have sex with me?"

Cashol's throat works again. "My Meh-gan, I want it more than anything." There's such an ache of yearning in his voice that it makes me shudder deep inside.

He must have some sort of mental hang-up about sex, I decide. Like he finds it unpleasant or dirty and doesn't want to spoil things. I roll onto my side, releasing his hand, and he hesitates before putting his hand on his knee, almost as if he's reluctant to let me go. He wants me. He wants this. His cootie is so loud it's practically drowning out the drums.

"We don't have to have sex right away," I tell him, and lean forward. I feel like a seductress, the vixen seducing the virgin. "But I don't like the thought of you hurting. We can help each other out, at least? Would you like that?"

I can see the war in his eyes. It's obvious that he wants to hold back, and even more obvious that he wants me to touch him. I lift a hand and he practically strains to raise his body to it.

"You don't have to be afraid of wanting this," I whisper. "I'll be gentle with you. I won't do anything you don't want to do."

"Meh-gan," he groans. "You...you do not have to touch me."

"You're right," I agree. "I don't have to do a thing." I gently place a hand on his shoulder and push him onto his back. "But if I want to do something, will you let me?"

Cashol groans again, as if in pain. "Yes."

I smile at him and get on my hands and knees. My hair swings forward, into my face, and I absently push it behind my ears. I grab the edge of the fur blanket covering him from the waist down and begin to peel it away, keeping my gaze locked on him. If there's the slightest hesitation in Cashol's eyes, I'll stop in an instant.

But all I see is blazing lust, and utter hope. It makes me feel sexy to see how much I affect him. I feel powerful, in control, and after weeks and weeks of uncertainty, it's the headiest feeling in the world. I'm achingly wet, too, and that just adds to my pleasure. I toss the fur aside when he doesn't stop me, and then sit on my knees next to him, looking him over.

This is *my* mate.

Cashol's body is huge, all lanky limbs that are somehow muscular and strong. He's big and powerful, but not in a way that seems brutish or overwhelming. Just...perfect for me, really. His belly moves with his panting breaths, his stomach flat enough to show off rippling abs, and I trail my fingers down his abdomen even as I gaze lower.

His loincloth looks as if it's at capacity. The man's simply enormous and I've never seen such a large bulge. Even knowing I had my hand on it earlier doesn't make it seem any less huge right now. He's rock hard and straining against the leather, and his leg muscles look tight. Even his nice feet—really nice, honestly—have curled toes, as if it's taking all of his focus not to grab my hand and start blasting away against my grip.

And oh man, do I find that thought enticing. In fact, I'm finding all of this enticing. I'm so turned on that I can feel how wet I am just by squeezing my thighs together. Everything feels hot and slick and needy and it's somehow the best feeling in the world. I clench my pussy even as I reach for one of the ties on his loincloth. "Can I touch you?"

His eyes look so, so dark a shade of blue that it makes me ache. "Do you want to?"

What a silly question. Of course I want to touch him. The cootie is making sure of that. But I understand what he's asking—he wants to make sure I'm doing this because I want to touch him, not because the cootie is making me. And while the cootie has me all amped up, there's a heady pleasure in being the first one to touch such a big, gorgeous body. The first one to show him what it's like when his cock is touched by a lover...and more.

I'm greedy with the thought of blowing his mind. I want to do this for him, more than anything. So I smile and tug one of the ties free. I flick the leather aside, and then his big, flushed cock is free, straining in the air, and I let out a little sigh of pleasure at the sight of it.

Ridges.

I didn't feel that yesterday when I palmed him through the leathers—or if I did, I didn't realize what it was I was touching.

Looking at him now, I can't stop smiling. I swear, the man's built like a girl's dirtiest dream. He's long and achingly thick, a vein tracing between the ridges that striate his cock. The head is plump and dark, wet with pre-cum, and just above his shaft rises a finger-length protrusion. The spur. Georgie has spoken enthusiastically about such things. Marlene, too. Actually, everyone has, now that I think about it. There's not a single complainer in the bunch that's resonated, which is a good sign.

Along with those ridges. Those ridges are a very good sign, too.

"You are staring," Cashol says, and there's laughter in his voice, and a hint of nervousness, too. "Is it much uglier than you are used to?"

I grin up at him. "Are you fishing for compliments? Do I need to tell you that you have a glorious dick?"

"I would enjoy hearing such things," he admits, that playful look on his face. "You can even lie to me."

"Oh, there's no need to lie," I tell him, breathless as I slide my body lower. "It's honestly mouth-wateringly impressive."

"Mouth-watering?" His mouth quirks, as if he's trying to decide whether to laugh or to frown. "It makes you hungry? Do you need dinner? I am happy to feed my mate." He looks eager at the thought.

At first I think this is more foreplay, and I get all hot and bothered. It's only when he looks over at the tray of food that I realize...he really means to feed me, and it has nothing to do with his cock.

I tilt my head.

Is he...being clueless to be funny? Or does he genuinely not know what I mean when I say he's mouth-watering? "I'll eat food later," I say specifically, and then sidle over on the floor until I'm near his big legs. I push his thighs apart, even though I really want to slide lower and stare at his feet for a few minutes. I...might have a thing for men's feet. Big, long, muscular feet just fascinate me, and Cashol has the biggest feet I've ever seen, and the most perfectly formed. No, I tell myself. Save the kooky foot stuff for later, when he's less virginal. I need to break him in easy.

And I decide I'm going to break him in with a blow job.

I sit between his legs, and when he tries to sit up, I gently push him back down again. "I said I was going to touch you, remember?"

"Yes, but..." He frowns, obviously a little stymied.

"You really are new to this, aren't you?" I smile up at him, tracing a finger down his flat abdomen. His skin really does feel like suede, and I kind of want to just rub him all over for the tactile pleasure of it.

"I know how mating works," he scoffs, a hint of a smile on his face. "I have seen it many times."

"In the wild?"

"In the cave, too. My people are not ashamed to mate, and sometimes it is unavoidable to catch someone." He shrugs. "And hunters talk. I know all about my role."

"Your role?" I try to stay straight-faced, but he really is cute like this. "What exactly is your role?"

"To pleasure you." The look on his face goes from laughing to intense. "To slide my mouth between your thighs and lick your cunt until you cry out. There is no taste better than a resonance mate on a hunter's tongue."

My thighs clench together. Oh god, just the visual of that makes me all needy. I definitely want that. I've only ever met one guy that willingly went down on me—but he was a cheater and we never stayed together. After that, it's been dud after dud in the bed. If Cashol thinks it's his duty to lick me to an orgasm, I am totally, completely, utterly fine with that. "Good. Then you should know I plan on doing the same to you."

His cock jerks, fresh beads of pre-cum sliding down the head. The breath hisses from between his teeth, and all the laughter seems to die away from him. "You...you will do that to me?"

"Why wouldn't I?"

"Humans do that to their males?"

Man, it's a good thing I like giving head or I'd be kicking myself right now. He's so utterly trainable. I can tell him everything I want in bed and he'll be eager to provide it to me. Holy shit. I've always been the one begging for the guy to get me off, to pay a little more attention here, to touch this spot a little more, and I always felt like a bit of a beggar. I'm starting to see why everyone around here is so thrilled for resonance. It's more than just a place to stay.

His dick is a damn sex toy and he feels morally obligated to lick pussy. This may be an ice planet, but it might also be a little slice of heaven.

I smile at Cashol. "Tell me if I do something you don't like."

"I do not think such a thing exists," he admits, gaze on me as if utterly fascinated.

10

MEGAN

*H*e sure makes it easy to flirt with him.

I sit back on my heels and pull my tunic over my head, deciding to move things along. He sucks in a breath at the sight of my naked breasts. I know from experience and being around the other women that the sa-khui females don't have breasts like we do. Theirs are mostly flat muscle, though I'm told that they grow larger when nursing. Maylak is heavily pregnant and she's got a decent rack to go with an enormous belly. I know mine looks a lot different, though. I know I have an okay face, but I've got a great body, and I can safely say my tits are first class. I cup them, enjoying his stare. "What do you think? I know they're different than you expect. Is that okay?"

"More than okay," he breathes. "Everything with you is perfect, Meh-gan."

"Flatterer," I tease, and lean over him. Or stretch, rather. I move catlike, crawling up his body in nothing but my loincloth, and press a light kiss to his mouth. I can't help but notice that his cock brushes against my belly as I lean in, and leaves a wet trace on my skin.

He groans against my mouth, gripping my arms and trying to deepen the kiss.

"Let me play," I whisper against his mouth. "You can touch me later."

"Later. Of course." He closes his eyes and thumps the back of his head against the cave wall. Cashol flexes his hands, as if he wants to touch me now and has to remind himself not to, and I admit, I like it. It makes me want to lean into my seductress role even more. I kiss his chin, then move downward, utterly aware of my body as my breasts bob free and his cock brushes against my skin. I lean in and kiss my way down his chest, and when the angle becomes too awkward—and his cock is too much in the way—I stop kissing and just wiggle down until I'm eye level with the beast itself.

"You know, I touched you earlier but I didn't realize how impressive you are," I whisper to him as I curl my fingers around his length. The breath hisses from his throat, and when I look up, his head is tilted back, resting against the cave wall, but his eyes are open. It's like he can't bear to let a single moment of this go without watching it.

It makes me feel powerful, too. I'm doing this to him. I'm a sex siren, a goddess of pleasure, and I feel like I've gone from unwanted Megan to something new with the snap of my fingers...or the purr of my cootie.

I bend down over him, letting my mouth whisper over the head of his cock in the barest of caresses. Not much, just enough to let him feel my breath and my lips. The taste of pre-cum, hot and salty, touches my tongue and I lick my lips, appreciating his flavor.

Cashol groans, loud and strong. "Your mouth..."

"Pretty good, isn't it?" I swipe my tongue against the underside of his cock, licking him like an ice cream.

That makes him huff with strangled laughter. "It is the best thing I have ever felt. I never imagined this, and now I feel like my mind is lacking."

"Why lacking?" I curl my fingers tighter around his base and gently lick up and down his length, learning the ridges of his cock with my tongue and my lips.

"Because..." he pants, shifting his weight over, and I glide my tongue over his skin. It's like he can't sit still while I caress him, because it's too much. He's panting, his muscles tense, and when I close my mouth around him, he grunts.

"Because?" I prompt, lifting my head. I drag my tongue over the crown of him again, deliberately dragging it slow and obvious so he can watch my movements.

He groans again. "Because I have thought of many ways to take you..." He pauses to grunt, his hips flexing as if he wants to push into my mouth. "I have imagined you on your back, and on your front, and even sitting on my face, but I have never, ever imagined this."

I moan at hearing that from him. He imagined me sitting on his face? For a virgin that doesn't know what a blow job is, that's a pretty graphic mental image...and I am all for it. I squeeze my thighs again, but it's not doing as much to ease the ache deep inside me. I'm so wet that the insides of my thighs feel coated with my juices, and my cootie's purring so hard it's making me vibrate in all kinds of interesting ways. "You...thought about me sitting on your face?"

"Mmm...yes." He bucks up against my mouth again, and I lick him. "Many, many times."

"Today? Or earlier than that?"

"Earlier," he pants, and I reward him with another hard suck of the head of his cock. "Ah, Meh-gan, your mouth..."

"Should I stop?"

"Never. Never. But..." A shudder wracks him. "I do not know how long I can last if you keep doing that."

"The idea isn't for you to last, silly," I say, letting my breath move over him again. I give him another long, explicit lick. "The idea is to make you come. Make you feel good." I look up, my mouth hovering over his cock. "But if you want me to stop—"

His hand reaches out and he grabs my hair, pushing my head down until my lips hit the head of his cock. Immediately, he jerks back, growling low in his throat. "I—I did not mean to do that—"

"It was sexy," I tell him. "I don't mind. You can do it again."

Cashol immediately plunks his hand back down on the back of my head, his fingers twisting in my hair.

I fight back my smile and return to licking his cock. I treat it like a delicious popsicle for a while, just giving it long, loving licks and enjoying the feel of my tongue moving over the ridges. I avoid his spur because I'm not entirely sure what to do with it just yet, and I'm sticking to what I know I'm good at. When he starts to push on my head ever so slightly, I give in and let him ease my head down as I take his cock in my mouth. I try to flatten my tongue to take as much of him in as possible, but he's so big and thick it feels like I'm choking on him if I go deeper than just a few inches. I breathe through my nose, relaxing my jaw, and do my best to suck and lick, and settle for just bobbing back and forth, letting the pressure of his hand shuttle my head against his cock.

His breath comes in short, jerky little inhales, and I know he's close. The taste of him is everywhere, his cock constantly leaking, and I can feel his body vibrating and tense. It's like he's ready to snap and just waiting for the right moment. I'm not afraid of him busting in my mouth, though—I kind of want it. Maybe it's the cootie, but I'm really liking his taste. It's not as acrid and bitter as other blowjobs I've given in the past, and I'm so wet and needy that I'm making soft little noises in my throat as I try to take him down as far as I can. I'm determined to deep throat the man. I am.

Then, his cock hits the back of my throat, and I half-swallow reflexively. Cashol groans, and then his hand tightens on the back of my head and he thrusts into my mouth, driving deep when I try to pull back. Before I can lift my head, he's coming, spilling down my throat and on my tongue, and I release him with a pop, letting his seed trickle down my chin. I squeeze the base of his cock, working him with harder, rougher squeezes to try and milk his release for him, and his fingers tighten in my hair so hard that it pulls, just a little. I don't mind that.

I've driven him so far over the edge that he doesn't know what he's doing, and I love that.

When he finally finishes coming, my hands are covered in his release, the taste of him is humming through my mouth, and I wipe my chin with a clean spot on the back of my hands, and then proceed to lick my fingers clean.

His eyes are sated slits as he watches me. "Meh-gan, you…"

"Mmmhmm?" I smack one of my fingers deliberately.

"You are…I have no words for how incredible you are."

"That was pretty good," I tell him, and wiggle my hips just a little. I'm still aroused, still achy and needy myself, but I can wait for him to recover. Maybe now he won't be so gung ho to wait and keep talking about this "shy" business. A shy man wouldn't push my head down and drive deeper into my throat. A shy man wouldn't daydream about me riding his face, would he? A shy man would definitely be awkward right now, watching me lick his cum off my fingers, but Cashol's just regarding me with an utterly entranced expression, like he's never seen anything better.

Whatever this man is, it's not shy.

11

MEGAN

After I finish cleaning my hands, I lean forward and give him a brief kiss. Maybe it's the girl in me that wants to see how he reacts when I try to kiss him with cum-breath, but he kisses me back just as eagerly, just as hungry as before. He doesn't care about the taste on my lips, and that makes me sigh with pleasure. He's rapidly climbing the charts here, and is quickly becoming my best bed partner ever…and we haven't even had official sex yet.

I kiss him again, just because I'm feeling needy, and he brushes a lock of hair off my face. "My beautiful Meh-gan," he murmurs, gazing at me with a look of pure adoration.

"I'm going to grab a drink of water," I say, giving him one last peck on the lips before crawling over to the food and water set out for us. "You want anything? Hungry?"

"Hungry?" he echoes, and then a mischievous look curls his smile. "Ravenous."

Now my toes are the ones curling.

Cashol watches me with heavy-lidded eyes as I take a few bites of food and drink two cups full of water. I'm practically squirming as I do, because just the way he watches me turns me on. The beat of the drums—still going—pulses through me and only adds to my heightened arousal. I've never been more turned on in my life.

I really hope he doesn't want to just cuddle after this. I might scream if he suggests going slow one more time.

"Are you done eating?" he finally asks when I set down the cup.

I nod, and he gestures that I should come to him. I practically scramble over to his side, moving as close as I can to his big, naked form. My breasts brush up against him and I gasp at how good it feels. It makes me lean in even more, so, so eager to be touched.

He leans in close, brushing his nose against mine. "Hello," he murmurs.

"Hi." Please touch me. I want to shove my tits into those big, impressive hands, I'm aching so badly.

"Can I undress you?" he asks, leaning in to kiss me.

I fling my arms around his neck and slam my mouth against his, hungry. He kisses me, a chuckle escaping him, and then his hands go to my loincloth. He hisses when his fingers skate along the edge of it, because I'm so wet that I've soaked the darn thing. "Look at how juicy your cunt is for me," he says, and I practically come just hearing that.

"Please, please touch me," I whisper aloud, caressing his cheek. "I'm so turned on right now."

"From touching me?" He groans, then kisses me again even as he flings my loincloth aside. His hands cup my ass and flex, and he nips at my lower lip. "You are going to make me hard all over again, Meh-gan."

"Good," I breathe. "Good. I want that."

He groans again, and then kisses my neck, moving lower. "Lie back for me."

As if I have to be asked twice. Eager, I move onto my back on the furs, practically quivering with anticipation as he looms over me.

Cashol's big hands smooth over my shoulders, then slide down my arms. "You have a lot more curves than a sa-khui female," he admits. "It is fascinating to see."

"Boobs," I pant.

"What?" His eyes meet mine.

I grab one of his big hands and plant it right onto my left breast. Even just that touch makes me practically come out of my skin and I whimper with pleasure.

"Aaah. What can I do to them?" He moves his hand over my breast slowly, as if trying to determine the best way to touch me.

"Whatever you want," I manage. "Kiss. Lick. Bite. Squeeze. Don't care. It'll feel good." I'm panting as I rattle off his options. "You can shove your cock between them and fuck if you want to."

He groans, and then his head drops between my breasts, and all I see are horns and thick hair. "That is another thing I never imagined..."

"Stick with me. I'll show you things." I wiggle under him. "Just...please, touch me."

He rubs his nose in the valley between my breasts, and I let out a little needy cry when he slides over to the mound of one, brushing his lips against my skin. He kisses his way over, exploring slowly, and I feel like the biggest jerk in the world because I want to grab his head and push him over to my nipple, to just shove the darn thing into his mouth so he'll lick it and end this aching torture. His breath fans across skin as he hovers over my nipple and I arch, groaning.

Seriously. Why is he not touching my nipples? Didn't he

hear what I said? Panting, I open my eyes, and realize he's watching me with a hungry, sly expression on his face. He's teasing me. Oh god. That is so, so infuriating…and so, so sexy.

"So cruel," I mutter, and grab his horns, dragging his head down.

He chuckles, and then his lips close over the tip of one of my breasts and I swear, I nearly come unglued at that touch. I'm moaning loud, writhing under him, and when his other hand goes to capture my other breast, I can't take it. I'm a wild woman as he teases one breast with that glorious, ridged tongue, and then moves to the other. I babble his name and gasp and make all kinds of ridiculous noises, lost in my arousal, and so close to coming that I feel like I'll shatter if he doesn't push me over the edge soon.

As if he can read my mind, he gives my nipple a gentle pinch with his fingers and then begins to kiss lower on my belly.

"Oh god," I moan. "Oh Cashol, are you going to do that for me?"

He kisses all the way down my stomach and then eases one of my thighs over his shoulder. I'm so wet that the air feels cold the moment he parts them, my skin tingling with anticipation. Heck, all of me is tingling with anticipation.

"My mate," he murmurs. "This is the pleasure I have been waiting for."

I want to ask what it was he thinks I just did for him when he was deep in my throat, but then his mouth is on my pussy and the breath hisses from my throat. I spread my legs wide, hooking my other ankle around his side as he drags that strong, ridged tongue over my pussy. It's clear he's learning me with his mouth, exploring my folds and nuzzling the curls of my sex as he tries different touches. The tip of his tongue flicks against the entrance to my core and then he moans, his arms tightening around me.

"So good," he says between probing, deep licks. "You taste so good, Meh-gan."

I squirm against his tongue, trying to push it deeper. I'm so hollow inside, so achy. I want to be filled up so badly, to get this endless, exquisite torture over with and get the orgasm I so richly deserve. God, do I want that orgasm. "Fingers," I pant, even though I swore to myself I wouldn't push him. It seems that the moment the arousal hits, I turn into the pushiest of women. "Use your fingers, Cashol."

"Where?" He licks me again.

"Inside me."

One slips deep and I whimper, because it instantly feels so much better and it's still not enough. "More."

Just like that, he adds a second. He pulls out, then pushes in slowly. "You are so tight. So tight and wet." He groans, lifting his fingers to his mouth and sucking them clean before dipping them into my core once more. "I want to taste all of you."

I rock my hips, nearly coming out of my skin. "Please. Please."

He thrusts deep with his fingers again, and this time, his mouth lands on the holy grail—my clit. My legs jerk and spasm, and I cry out as he begins to circle it with the tip of his tongue, just like I'd shown him with his fingers earlier. It's too much, and I'm so worked up that the orgasm bursts through me, my entire body shivering and locking up. He groans and continues to work my clit, his fingers pushing into me with slick, wet noises. "Meh-gan," he growls, and he sounds so damn sexy. "Meh-gan. My Meh-gan."

A little sigh escapes me as I come down from my orgasm. I twitch every time his tongue strokes over my clit, his fingers pumping into me. "God, that was amazing." Just like that, he's at the top of the bed partner list.

My big blue mate growls again and looks up at me even as he licks my clit, his mouth buried between my thighs. I shiver all over again, wondering if I'm greedy enough to let him work me to another orgasm just like this. But eating each other out—no matter how incredible—won't help resonance. And Cashol has that heated look in his eyes as he gazes up at me.

"Are you hard again?" I ask him, breathless.

He nods, his tongue swiping against my skin in the most lewd and erotic movement ever. "Very."

"Still shy?"

Cashol gives me the most heated of looks, his eyes so intense it shivers up my spine. "No."

I tug on his arm. "Then come make love to your mate. Come and fill me up."

He leans over and bites the inside of my thigh, and a shudder ripples through me. "You want my cock in that hot, tight little cunt of yours?"

Oh god, I do now. I nod eagerly, tugging on his horns. "Yes. God, yes."

He moves up over me, looming enormous as he leans in and kisses me. "Are you sure, my mate? I can hold out—"

But why? I put a hand to his cheek and kiss him, hard, even as I wrap my legs around him. "Now, Cashol. Please."

He nods, and then his big body stiffens as he puts a hand between my thighs, guiding his cock to my entrance. His gaze is locked to my face, as if he's waiting for me to scream for him to stop, to tell him to hold off, but I want this so badly. I need his cock. It doesn't matter that I just had the best orgasm of my life —I'm pulsing with anticipation and ready for another. "Give me a baby," I whisper.

Give me security.

Cashol groans, and instead of inching into me as I expect him to do as a *shy* man, he thrusts deep. I suck in a breath as he pushes himself to the hilt inside me, and his spur rubs right into place next to my clit.

He freezes on top of me, every muscle tensing. "Meh-gan? Are you...did I hurt you?"

I'm overwhelmed for a moment, my head buzzing as if my brain has fried. He's so big, so deep and big that I feel as if my entire body is adjusting for his length. I've dated guys that didn't feel like much of anything inside me, but oh god, this is not like that at all. He's so big and thick that every nerve ending feels as if it's twitching right now, and when he shifts his weight over me, his spur rubs against the side of my clit.

Did I think the last orgasm was the best one ever? I think I'm about to be proven wrong.

"Meh-gan?" Cashol's panting, worried, his face contorted with strain. Even so, he reaches up and gently brushes his knuckles over my cheek. "Should I move?"

I moan at the thought. "Yes. Move. Moving is good." He slides out of me and I yelp, clinging to his shoulders. "No, no—move inside me."

Cashol hesitates. "I am not hurting you?"

"Fuck no." I arch my hips, trying to encourage him to return. Now that he's gone I feel so damn hollow. "Come back. I want you."

He groans and then his hand is back between us, brushing over my core a split second before he thrusts deep again. I gasp, my nails digging into his suede-soft skin.

"Oh fuck, that's really good," I whisper. "Oh, Cashol."

"I am here," he tells me, and sinks deep again, as if he's a damn natural. I suck in a little breath with his next thrust, and then it's like he can't stop himself. He repeats himself over and over again. "Here," he murmurs. "Here. Here." With every word, he pumps deep into me, and then he's moving faster and harder, until we're slamming up against each other. "Here, Meh-gan."

I put a hand to the back of his neck. "I have you."

He groans and pushes deeper, one hand locking at my hips.

It feels like he's bottoming out, hitting so deep that there's a twinge of pain with the pleasure, but I'm so wrapped up I don't care. He's shuttling so fast that I can't possibly keep up with moving my hips, so I just arch against him and hold on for the ride.

Cashol makes a choking sound, his body stiffening over me, and when a hot warmth floods my insides, I realize that he's come already, and I'm left hanging. I stroke his back, murmuring sweet words to him as he clenches, lungs moving like bellows, through the orgasm. He finally collapses on top of me and my thighs twitch, because I'm so close to my own release…but I guess that's just greedy.

When Cashol catches his breath, he lifts his head and peppers my face with small kisses. "You are perfect. So perfect."

I smile at him, doing my best not to wriggle up against the spur that's jabbing me just so. "Not shy anymore?"

"Not shy, no." He lets out a tired laugh, then pauses. "Did you…"

"It's fine," I tell him brightly. "There will be other times."

A look of disappointment crosses his face. His hand moves between us, and his gaze meets mine. "May I touch you?"

Oh. I love that he offers. I love that he thinks about my pleasure, about getting me off a second time even when I just came not too long ago. I let my legs fall as far apart as I can and nod, and shiver against him when his fingertips brush my clit. It doesn't take long for me to come again, my hands buried in his hair, my face pressed against his neck as he teases my oversensitized flesh with little flicks until I'm there.

Then it's my turn to collapse in my mate's arms.

He pulls me close against him, his lips brushing over my skin as he holds me tight. I should probably get up and clean up, but I'm not in a hurry. It's nice to just lie here and be cuddled for a bit.

A low thrumming settles in my chest, and I realize I'm still humming. Still resonating. I guess it'll take a few more tries. Cashol's hand strokes my cheek, then moves down my arm. He lazily traces his fingers over my elbow, then boldly moves to cup my breast, his thumb teasing my nipple into a point again.

"Do you think the drums will ever stop?" he muses. "They have better stamina than I do."

I giggle. "But once the drums finish, they're done and put away. Meanwhile, you're ready again almost instantly." I can already feel him hardening against my hip. "So don't knock your stamina too much."

He just grins at me. "As long as you are not disappointed, I am happy."

"No. Not disappointed."

Not disappointed at all.

12

CASHOL

Everyone in the cavern is helping themselves to medicinal tea the next morning, talking in low voices, and sleeping in. I want nothing more than to strut through the cave and bask in the admiration of my fellow hunters, but I will hear their teasing words some other time. Instead, I watch my lovely Meh-gan sleep, curled up in the furs at my side, her yellow mane spilling over the blankets.

So much for going slow.

I hope my chief is not very disappointed in me. I tried to go slow with her, I truly did. Meh-gan would not be denied, though, and I am a weak hunter in the face of such enthusiasm. Last night, she used her mouth and her hands in ways I could scarcely believe, and I tried to do the same for her. By the time we fell asleep shortly before dawn, we had mated at least seven times, and our khuis slowed their song, indicating that resonance was fulfilled.

I am a little disappointed it went so fast. I know others

resonate for days on end, and I think perhaps that would be grand. Tiring, but grand.

I wake Meh-gan with a kiss to her shoulder. I love kissing her. It does not matter if my mouth mates with hers or not—I want to touch her all over and just stroke her soft skin. I want her scent in my nose...and her taste on my tongue, her hands on my body. My cock rises stiffly once more, but Meh-gan only burrows deeper into the blankets, smacking her lips.

"Shall I get food for us?" I whisper, nuzzling her neck as she tries to sleep. "And perhaps some hot tea?"

She shrugs, sleepy, and I decide that is close to a "yes." The thought of providing for my new mate fills me with glee, so I dress quickly and rake my hand through my mane, trying to comb it out with my fingers. I emerge from the cave to see Sevvah grinning in my direction. She has a plate full of freshly cooked kah cakes and I bound over to her.

"My favorite elder," I tease.

She shakes her head at me. "Look at you. You are a mess." She licks one finger and tries to smooth down a bit of my mane. "What will your pretty mate think if she sees you look like this?"

"She will think I do not care what my mane looks like because I am too busy satisfying her?"

Sevvah snorts. "I have a gift for your mate. I was digging through my supplies and found some old tunics she might like. Come. I will make some tea, too."

I hesitate, glancing back at the entrance to the supply cave—my cave, I amend. The cave I will live in with my mate. The thought fills me with pride and a curious sense of joy. Ever since the khui sickness took my father, I bounced from cave to cave. After the sickness ravaged the tribe, there were many of us left without family, and while the elders did what they could, it was not the same as having a family. The only person I had left was my cousin Vektal, but he had taken over being chief, and was constantly busy. I remember many nights I sat by Sevvah's fire, trying to seem lighthearted and full of joy so I would not be a burden.

She is as close to a mother as I can remember, so I let her fuss over me and even though I long to go and curl up around my mate again, I go to Sevvah's cave and let her fuss over me.

By the time I emerge from Sevvah's cave, I have a basket full of goods for my new home with my mate, a pouch of tea leaves, a morning meal for my female, and a waterskin full of hot, fresh tea. It feels as if it takes forever to get back to her, but when I return to our cave, Meh-gan is gone.

It is...disappointing.

I set down my burdens and glance around the cave, but I do not see my yellow-maned mate's head. Frowning to myself, I notice Haeden near the main entrance, and head over there. I had promised to go on a long hunt with him, but things have changed.

Everything has changed.

I cannot stop smiling as I approach, and the moment Haeden sees me, he rolls his eyes and goes back to strapping additional spear-shafts to his pack. "Ho, my friend," I call, in a cheery mood. "The weather is lovely this morning, is it not? A perfect day for a hunt."

He grunts. "I would ask you how your evening went, but we know," Haeden grumbles. "We *all* know."

I clap a hand on his back. "Resonance is glorious. I never thought I would have such joy, and here I am." I shake my head in wonder. "You will be going on that hunt by yourself."

"You did not fulfill resonance? I am surprised." He shakes his head, tightening a strap. "You kept me up all night with your grunting. And if it was not you, it was Vektal, or Dagesh."

He has a sour look on his face. "This cave needs thicker walls."

I chuckle, because he is simply mad that his furs remained empty last night. I know my friend and I know he is happy for me...even if it means he must go hunting alone. He is simply going to frown about it for a bit first. I flick his braid. "We fulfilled resonance, thank you." I rub my chest, where my khui sings softly now, as if it is tired. "But things are still new. I wish to stay near Meh-gan for a while. I do not want her to miss me too much."

Haeden snorts. "She will only miss you if you are gone."

I want to tease him back, to say that he is jealous, but I hold my tongue. Haeden's sad history is not something to be thrown in his face, ever. I am too good of a friend to be cruel, so I just grin at him. "You are right. I am the one that would miss her if I was to go out for many nights. I do not want to wake from a dream in which I kiss my mate only to find I am kissing your ugly face instead."

"I think *neither* of us wishes that."

I glance around the cave. People are moving about, projects being spread in open space. Sevvah and Kemli are talking, and a fresh pouch of tea is being placed over the fire by Hemalo while Harrec laughs and gestures about something to one of the human females. I still do not see Meh-gan. "Have you seen my mate?"

"Yes. She ran for the distant hills at dawn," Haeden grumbles.

I mock-kick a bit of snow onto his boot. "At dawn, my mouth was still on her."

My friend raises a hand into the air. "Spare me your bragging. She disappeared with the noisy one a short time ago. So you will not go hunting with me?"

"Not this time. Perhaps the next." I cross my arms over my chest, considering. I normally love to go out on a long hunt, but

I feel no urge to do so right now. I want to spend time with Meh-gan. I want to hear her laugh. I want to see her smile.

I want to mate with her again.

I will definitely be staying close to the cave for the near future. My cousin Vektal will understand. He, too, has a new mate and has been swapping longer hunts for quicker ones. I will set trap lines nearer to the caves and hope for the best. I gesture toward the center of the cave. "You could always ask Harrec if he wishes to go."

Haeden gives me an unimpressed look. "I would rather go alone."

I talk to Haeden a bit longer, then begin looking for my mate again. If she was with her friend Jo-see, the "noisy" one that Haeden refers to, they will not be far. Both Meh-gan and Jo-see always seem to be working on one project or another in the caves, and rarely venture out. I check one of the storage caves, and then I hear a feminine giggle as I move toward the females' cave. Of course. Jo-see lives in that cave, and Meh-gan did until last night, when we resonated.

Just thinking about her makes me smile, and I rub my chest. I move along the wall, curious to hear the murmur of voices. I can make out Meh-gan's chuckle, and Jo-see's higher-pitched giggle.

"You can have all the leather straps," Jo-see is saying. "You know I don't want them."

"Are you sure?" Meh-gan teases. "You can always make a ball gag for your buddy Haeden."

They both giggle. "Ball gags are for sex, and the last thing I want to do is think about sex with that man. Yuck." She makes a disgusted sound. "He's such an ass."

Well now, I wish to know what a ball gag is. I am very curious, because now that I have Meh-gan as my mate, I am interested in all things sex.

"He's really not that bad," Meh-gan says, the sounds of rustling coming from within the cave. "Cashol is friends with him."

"Oh my god, look at your face when you say his naaaaame," Jo-see erupts in giggles. "That's sooo cute. Are you happy, then?"

"I mean...I guess? Define happy?"

I frown to myself. Why is her answer not instantly "yes"? Mine would be. Is she not full of joy this morning, as I am? I hide deeper in the shadows, listening.

"How was resonance? Are you in love?"

"After one night? Not quite. We still barely know each other. He's really nice, but I feel a little guilty. He wanted to go slow with things and I talked him out of it."

"Because the cootie was pushing you?" Jo-see giggles again.

"No, because I won't be safe here until I'm pregnant."

"Well, problem solved," Jo-see calls triumphantly. "You are now officially pregnant."

I move away from the cave, because I do not want to hear any more. I am...oddly hurt. Meh-gan did not sound as if she wanted to mate with me at all. Strangers? How can we be strangers after last night? We shared everything. I have never felt so close to another as I did when I held her in my arms.

But for her...it was duty. She did not want to go slow, because she wanted to fulfill resonance. Because for some reason, she thinks the sa-khui will abandon her.

My pride is wounded, I decide. I wanted to be enough for her. I wanted her to be so entranced with our mating that she would be all smiles this morning—and every morning from now on. But Meh-gan must need more to feel secure. She thinks she will be abandoned if she does not please me. Vektal was right in that I should have gone slow, but I did not listen. I let my cock make the decisions—my cock, and my mate's eager hands.

Now I know why she was so eager, and I feel foolish. I head to my cave, grab a spear and leather rope, and decide that there is no better time than now to set up my trap lines near the cave.

Perhaps a long walk will clear my head.

13

MEGAN

*I*t's funny. I thought resonance would solve all my problems. I thought once I resonated, I'd be so bowled over with everything that all my anxieties would go away. I'd be so blown away with lust for my mate and happiness with the pregnancy that I'd finally feel like part of the tribe and I could stop worrying over everything.

Hasn't happened.

I feel the same this morning as I did yesterday morning, but now everything in my unstable world has changed again.

I head back to my cave after filling a basket with leather cord. I chatted with Josie a bit, but her enthusiasm and rosy view of my new mating just makes me feel worse. Why aren't I completely in love with Cashol overnight? She thinks I am, no matter that I hint otherwise. She still thinks resonance will solve everything. Maybe it will in time, but I still feel the need to show I can be a good, hard worker. So...macramé it is.

When I get back to my new cave, Cashol is nowhere to be

seen. There's some new stuff in baskets, a plate of food, and a tea pouch hanging over the coals of the fire, but Cashol isn't here. I glance back outside into the main cave and don't see him anywhere, so I sit down to eat. Maybe he'll be back soon.

But as time passes and Cashol doesn't return, I feel...hurt. Stupid. Why did I think he'd want to spend the day with me? I tie a few cords to the bone macramé ring, loop it onto my big toe, and start to braid the belt I've decided to make for my new mate. His is faded and worn, and I noticed it slung low on his hips and he had to hitch it up more than once. A new belt would look good on him, and this is something I can do. So I weave the leather cords, letting my mind wander, and wonder what I did wrong.

He'd hinted that he wanted to spend time with me today, but the moment he had the chance, he left. Is it...me? Did I do something wrong? Am I annoying to be around? I think of last night, and how incredibly hot the sex was. How despite the initial "shyness" of my mate, we were all over each other until dawn. Once resonance was fulfilled, I thought maybe that'd be the end of it, that I wouldn't be all that interested in another round, but I find myself thinking about his feet, and his big hands, and his goofy smile that stretches his narrow face.

Cashol is really cute.

Just thinking about him makes me ache. I really want this to work. Maybe I was too pushy last night? Maybe I need to give him space? He's been living on his own for a long time. Maybe having me around is going to be hard for him. That...sucks. If he needs time, I need to give it to him, though.

As I weave the leather cords, I come up with a plan. It's similar to the current plan of "work hard and make everyone in the cave like me" plan. With Cashol, I'll be the same. I'll give him space and stay busy. I'll be so agreeable and such a good homemaker he'll realize that it's nice to be around me. That he doesn't have to run off at dawn—I'll give him space, even if I don't want to.

And then maybe all of this will work out. I hope.

CASHOL

By the time I've set my last trap, I have a plan in place.

I am going to have to seduce my mate. Not in the furs—it is clear we are very compatible when it comes to that. But her words to Jo-see still ring in my ears. She does not know if she is happy. She does not feel secure.

As her mate, it is my job to ensure that she is both. And I want her to fall in love with me. I want her to give me her heart. So I must be the most attentive male ever. I must shower her with affection, make her laugh and blush. I should spend every moment I can with her, and that means no long hunting trips.

None of this is a hardship, truly. Already I miss her. I wonder if she has spent the day with Jo-see and the other females, laughing and enjoying herself, or if she misses me? Has she thought about me at all?

Has she thought about mating again?

Because I have thought about it. A lot. Coming together with her was incredible in all ways. I rub my mouth, hungry for another taste of her...but Vektal was right. I pushed too hard and did not realize she was wanting to mate to ensure her safety here. I cannot push her into more matings. They must be her idea. I will simply wait for her to approach me, then. Meh-gan is a bold enough female—last night was evidence of that—and so if she wishes to mate, she will simply show me.

I just have to wait for her signal.

Resolved, I return to the cave, my traps laid and my leather boots wet from the snow. It is late enough that I have missed the evening meal, but next time I will not have to take quite so long when I go out. Perhaps Meh-gan will want to check traps with me? I like the thought of spending the day with her, seeing her nose grow pink with cold as we trek through the snow.

Perhaps we will stop at a hunter cave and she will let me lick her cunt until she tries to pull my horns off again. I grin to myself at the thought. Last night, ahhhh. Last night was the best night of my life.

I want so many more nights like last night.

I do not see my mate as I cut through the main cavern, so I bound through, moving past cookfires and heading straight for my cave. The privacy screen is up and I hesitate for a moment. Do I go inside? Or do I leave it as it is? After a pause, I push my way in, deciding to chance it.

Meh-gan is inside, knotting and weaving one of her leather projects. She looks up as I enter, a beaming smile on her face. "Hey, you."

"Hello, pretty one. Did you have a good day?"

"It was great," she says enthusiastically. "I got so much done. It was nice and quiet in here and I was able to work undisturbed."

I keep smiling, but her answer is...distressing. She got so much done because I was gone? That is not the answer I wished to hear. But I want her to feel as if she is free to do as she chooses. "I am glad. I set down a bunch of traps, myself." I strip off my wet boots and spread them on stones near the fire. "It was a good day to go hunting. Nice weather."

"Very nice weather," she agrees, and then we both fall silent again.

This is not how I imagined talking to my mate when I returned. I hoped to be greeted with enthusiastic mouth-matings, declarations of how much she missed me...and instead, we are speaking of the weather.

I watch as her nimble fingers work, trying to think of something to say. Nothing comes to mind, and I sit in silence, wishing I could think of easy words to say to her. Why is it I can think of things when I wish to flirt, but the moment she becomes my mate, my mind goes blank? "Would you like to go hunting with me in the morning?" I blurt out.

She pauses, thinking, and looks over at me. "You want me to go hunting with you?"

"Yes. It would be a good opportunity for you to learn." She seems so very eager to learn everything lately.

Meh-gan smiles, but it seems more polite than enthusiastic. "Of course I'd love to go. Thank you for inviting me."

She is nice...and yet she feels remote. I do not know what to make of it, and I think of her conversation with Jo-see.

I won't be safe here until I'm pregnant.

Now that she is pregnant, is she...tired of me? I smack my fist against my brow, frustrated with myself. I should have wooed her like Vektal said, not jump into the furs at the first opportunity. I have messed everything up.

I must somehow slow everything down.

I look around the small cave. I see the furs, neatly made, and it looks like far too small a space to share with someone if I am to be going "slow." There is enough room for both of us, but I know I will end up touching her. I will reach for her soft curves and her glorious teats, I will brush against her pale skin and then I will be utterly lost. There is a bundle of furs in the back of the cave, and I leap to my feet and grab them.

Separate furs. That is how we slow things down.

Proud of myself for thinking of it, I gesture at the furs happily. "Look. We have enough for two sets. That means we do not have to share."

She blinks at it for a moment, and then puts another one of those blank smiles on her face. "Great."

I am not sure if she is pleased, or sad. It is so hard to tell with her, because she gives me the same polite smile for everything.

14

MEGAN

We don't go hunting the next morning, and I can't say I'm disappointed. I know my strengths, and I'm pretty sure hunting isn't one of them, but I can't exactly turn it down. Not after Cashol pointed out how much I could "learn." I feel as if he's quietly chiding me for not pulling my weight, so I work extra hard while sitting around the fire, sewing tunics and working on belts for so long that my eyes get tired and the tips of my fingers blister and callus from holding a needle. I take my turn cooking and I scrub at laundry. I help Hemalo and Kashrem clean skins. I clean roots and dice them. I dry leaves for the hot tea everyone loves.

And I never, ever complain.

The weather is super snowy for the next few days, and Cashol explains to me, with his big, goofy grin, that he doesn't want to take me out on a day that it's going to be unpleasant and nasty. Humans are delicate, he reminds me every morning, and must be taken care of. So we don't hunt.

We don't share furs, either.

Other than that first night of resonance, Cashol avoids privacy with me. He sets up his own set of furs across from mine and never does more than give me a quick peck on the forehead goodnight. Here I was thinking we'd had the best sex I'd ever had, and certainly better than I'd hoped when I got kidnapped from Earth, and he's acting like he's done with me. It reminds me of the guy I met at the club who slept with me and then disappeared when he went "out to get coffee for breakfast" and never returned. I told myself that it didn't matter. That it was just a one-night stand and my feelings weren't hurt. Except they were, and that hurt lingered when I wound up pregnant. How was I ever going to explain to my baby that I didn't know his dad's name?

Not that it matters now, because that baby's just a painful, sad memory I'll carry with me forever.

It does hurt that I'm here on a strange planet a million, billion, trillion miles from my own and I'm still getting the cold shoulder. At first, I wonder if I've hurt Cashol's feelings. I do my best to be smiley and agreeable, and try to be the ice planet version of a happy homemaker. Cashol is cheery and sweet and funny just like usual...and just goes to his own furs every night. I don't understand it.

The next two weeks are the longest two weeks of my life. It snows every day. He goes hunting every day. I work until I can't keep my eyes open, and smile and pretend to be a happy newlywed. I giggle at all the teasing the other women do, and inside, I'm dying a little more every day. What's so wrong with me that no one can love me? What's so awful about me in particular that makes men run away?

I bury my hurt under a smile and keep going, because what else can I do?

I must be pregnant now, though. The resonance sounds my

khui makes have softened and lost that urgent call. Now, I purr ever so slightly around Cashol, as if my khui is acknowledging his nearness, but that's it. There's no wild pressure to mate, no intense urgency, no frantic need...which means I must be pregnant. Maybe that's why Cashol sleeps apart.

Or maybe it's just...me.

"Today, I think, we will go hunting," Cashol announces over morning tea.

I've just unrolled a length of leather straps for one of the belts I'm working on and do my best not to frown at him. "Do what?"

"Hunting," he says agreeably, moving to squat by my side. He's all smiles this morning, his mood chipper at the crack of dawn. "Remember? We are to hunt together so I can teach you how to set traps and check them."

"Hunting. Right. I forgot." I smile brightly even though I feel like screaming, and roll back up the leather for another time. "When do you want to go?"

"Now is a grand time."

"Sure is," I chirp at him. "So grand."

He gives me an odd look. "Do you not want to go hunting with me? I thought we might spend the day together."

Oh, so after two weeks of ignoring me and sleeping apart, now he wants to spend the day together? I don't understand him, and I feel a stab of resentment that he thinks I can blow hot and cold like this. "I'm good. Hunting will be fun. Let me get dressed."

I put on several layers of warm clothing as Cashol packs a bag, and throw on my heaviest boots. I normally wear "light" shoes inside the cave, but I have a heavier-duty pair for going out. Not that I go out. Even so, I feel uncertain as I tie another layer of wraps around myself and pull my hair into a braid. A quick glance over at Cashol shows he's not wearing more than a vest and the usual loincloth and leggings with his boots, as if this is a mild summer day instead of a snowy hellscape.

He beams at me, shrugging the pack onto his shoulder and grabbing his spear. "Are you ready?"

I gesture at my layers. "I sure hope so." There's really only one way to find out if it's warm enough, and that's heading out into the wild with him.

"Do not worry," he says reassuringly. "We will not go far."

IT'S SOON CLEAR TO ME THAT "NOT VERY FAR" IS DIFFERENT IN MY book than it is in Cashol's book. When I think "not far," I think maybe we'll head over to the next valley, or take a short jaunt over the nearest cliffs that this planet is riddled with. Cashol, however, sprints down trail after trail with boundless energy, his blue tail flicking. I struggle to keep up, having shorter legs and being burdened with heavy fur wraps...and the fact that I'm just not as athletic as he is.

"Not much farther," he says cheerfully, over and over again.

And yet we keep going. The snow gets deeper, the landscape changes around us, and still Cashol keeps on trekking, and I'm regretting my decision to go out with him. The cold chaps my cheeks and my legs ache from waddling through the deep snow. My boots are soaked and my toes feel like icicles, and I feel a stab of resentment for Cashol every time he looks over at me and smiles. Doesn't he realize how miserable I am?

Then again, probably not. Because I keep smiling despite my murderous thoughts. I act like I'm having a great time. I can't draw a deep breath, and I feel like I'm ready to collapse, but I pretend like that's no big deal.

"Do you need to stop?" he asks me when I lag behind him.

"No, I'm good," I wheeze. "We can keep going."

He gives me an uncertain look, but I tromp on past him, determined not to be the problem. He jogs back to my side, and then points at a cluster of the pink, flippy trees up ahead. "I have a few traps set there. Let us see what we have caught, eh?"

"Great," I echo. And it is. Maybe if we've caught something, we can go back to the cave already and I can relax. I don't see why Liz wants to constantly go hunting with Raahosh. I much prefer staying at the nice, warm cave and working on craft projects. This fresh air was nice for about five minutes, and then the cold set in.

I just don't think I'm much of an adventurer, and I worry that's going to disappoint Cashol. He looks like he's having the best time with me here at his side. He glances over at me and I beam at him, trying to look as if I'm having a better time than I am. It's not his fault I'm a couch potato at heart.

A wild, high-pitched shriek cuts through the air.

I gasp, clutching at Cashol's arm. "What the fuck was that?"

He chuckles at my surprise, squeezing my gloved hand. "It sounds as if we have caught something. Let us go and see."

My stomach clenches uneasily, but I nod. "All right."

Cashol leads the way, with me using his spear as a walking stick and keeping pace a short distance behind. There's a flurry of snow kicked up and then he bends down near a tree and gestures that I should join him.

"A nice, fat hopper. Still alive," he tells me. "Do you want to dispatch it?"

I swallow hard and go to his side. Sure enough, there's one of those fat, bunny-like hoppers. Their fur is coarser and thicker than a rabbit's and they're not as sweet faced. They're also a lot fatter and remind me of a roly-poly snow badger, and the most "rabbit-like" thing about them are the large back feet so they can spring through the drifts of snow.

They're good eating. In fact, the hunters bring them in all the time.

I just...never had to look one in the eye before.

The hopper gives another screech of pain, twisting in the trap-line. Normally, Cashol explained earlier, the trap-line loops the caught animal around the neck and they end up strangling themselves. This hopper is unluckier than most, because it's caught around one of his back legs and the snow around him is bloody from how much he's twisted at his bonds, and his leg hangs limp.

He's trapped.

I know just how he feels.

"One swift stab should do it," Cashol tells me helpfully.

I nod, the blood roaring in my ears. I can do this. I can do this. Everyone here hunts. It's the difference between life and death. I eat fresh meat all the time. Heck, I even eat it raw since my taste buds have changed since getting a khui. I've skinned things before. I've seen how the meat is prepared. I can do this.

I can.

I lift the spear, and my hands are sweaty in my gloves. I'm breathing hard and so tired that my hands are shaking. The sooner I get this thing dead, the sooner I can go back to the cave and just crawl into my furs.

Even so, I hesitate. I've never killed anything. Ever.

I know it has to be done...and yet.

I'm not sure I'm the one that can do it. I lift the spear, trembling, and stare down at the fat, fluffy, helpless creature as it lets out another too-human sounding cry of distress. If I want to be part of this tribe, part of this world, I have to fit in. There's no room for weakness. No room for sympathy.

It's me or this stupid hopper.

I have to prove I can do this.

"Make it quick," Cashol encourages me. "You can do it. My first kill was a hopper."

I hold the spear aloft, shaking. "H-how old were you?"

"Three or four turns of the seasons. Make your movement swift and sure when you bear down."

Three or four? And here I am, a grown-ass woman and I'm shaking like a leaf.

It gives one last, defeated little cry of pain and my throat closes.

I...can't do this.

I toss the spear aside and shake my head mutely. I'm not a killer. I'm just...not.

"You cannot leave it, Meh-gan," Cashol says, his voice gentle. "It will not survive with a wounded back leg. The kindest thing we can do for it is to give him a quick, good death."

I burst into tears and storm away.

At least, I try to. Instead, I just stumble in the thick snow and end up planting face-first into the powder, which only makes me cry harder. I sob uncontrollably, aware that I'm not just crying over that hopper, or having to kill it. I'm having an utter breakdown because no matter what I do, I'll never, ever fit in. I can't be the person these people want me to be. I can't be the mate Cashol needs, because I'm not Liz or Georgie, and I just cry harder.

Behind me, the hopper lets out another cry, only for it to be cut short by the crack of bones. It goes silent, and then I hear feet crunching in the snow. Cashol's hand brushes over my shoulder. "Meh-gan...are you all right, my mate?"

I just sob harder, sick at heart. Do I *seem* all right to him? Because I don't feel all right. I'm hysterical, and I'm cold, and tired, and terrified, and I can't even kill an ugly rabbit that probably would have bitten the shit out of me if I reached out to help it. The hopper isn't the problem; I'm the problem, and it's becoming more and more obvious with every day that passes.

I don't belong. I'll never belong.

Even Cashol doesn't want to sleep with me. One night with me, and he'd had enough.

15

MEGAN

I weep uncontrollably, burying my face in the snow like a child.

"Come, come," Cashol says in the gentlest voice. "Your tears hurt my heart, my mate." He rolls me onto my back, and when I can't bear to look him in the eye, scoops me up and carries me, bridal style. "Let us get out of this snow and get you near a fire."

I shake my head, because I can't imagine being carried back to the cave like a baby after one freaking day of hunting. No one will ever let me live this down and the tribe will make fun of me. "Please don't take me back just yet."

He considers for a moment, then changes directions, heading farther away from the main cave. "There is a hunter cave in this direction. We can rest there."

"Thank you," I tell him as I shift in his arms. I notice he's got his spears and his pack on his shoulder, and I feel like such an ass for letting him hold me. "I can walk."

"No."

Surely he can't mean to carry me the entire way to the cave? "Cashol—"

"I said no, Meh-gan," Cashol repeats, tone firm but gentle. "Allow me to carry my mate."

I let him carry me after that, because I really don't want to pick a fight over something I don't want to do. I'm achingly tired, and very aware at how out of shape I am compared to him. He's just bounded over these snowy hills like they're nothing, whereas it feels like an utter slog for me. It's just another thing for me to worry about. Like, what if the rest of the tribe feels I can't keep up and they leave me behind to die?

A fresh round of tears erupts and I bury my face against his neck.

"Please, do not cry, Meh-gan," Cashol murmurs as he walks. "I cannot stand it when you weep. If it was possible to let the hopper go, I would have, but it truly was not fair to release him wounded like that."

I just cry harder, because he really thinks I'm upset about the hopper. That I have such a tender heart that I can't handle killing things. Which...I do. But the tender heart is not the problem as much as I've been thrust into a society that I don't fit into, and I worry they'll find out I'm dead weight and get rid of me. I'm not as full of perseverance as Georgie, or as athletic as Liz. I'm not as sweet as Nora or as chatty as Josie. Ariana doesn't fit in well because she cries a lot, and I've seen the exasperated looks people toss in her direction.

I don't want those looks directed at me.

Each time I fail at something, I feel...awful. Worthless. And it just adds to the stress of fitting in. But I don't want Cashol to know that. I don't want anyone to know that I'm struggling. I just want to blend in and be happy.

So I swipe at the tears icing up on my cheeks and try to smile. "I'm fine. I'm fine."

"You are not fine," he argues, and I can hear the worry in his voice. "I did not realize you hated hunting so much. I feel responsible. You should have told me you did not like it and we would have done something else together."

My lower lip wobbles and now I feel even worse. He just wanted to spend the day with me? Here I've been thinking mean thoughts about him dragging me through the snow and he thought we were supposed to be having fun together. I burst into fresh tears and he holds me tighter.

"We are almost there," he reassures me. "All will be well."

That makes me smile, just a little. As if everything can be repaired by dragging me to a cave somewhere. If only it were that easy.

Sure enough, within the next few minutes, he grunts an apology as he sets me down, and then enters the cave to check it out. When he's assured that all is well, he pulls me in with him and then sets me down in front of a dark firepit. "You sit," he demands. He pulls a rolled up fur out of the back of the cave and drapes it over my shoulders, then pulls a bag of herbs from his pack. "I will make tea."

"I can make tea," I offer, reaching for the pouch in his grip.

He smacks the back of my hand. "What did I just say?"

I stare at him, astonished, and then let out a watery little giggle. "Did...you just smack me?"

"You are not a very good listener, Meh-gan," he chides me, squatting by the firepit. "When I say I will make my mate tea, I will make my mate tea."

"I just...don't want to be helpless. That's all."

"There is a difference between being helpless and letting someone do things for you," he says as he puts tea over the cold firepit and then fills the pouch with water from his skin. He sets to work making a fire, building it faster than I ever could, and I realize it's yet another thing I'm not good at—making fires. Another thing in the endless list of tasks I need to learn.

Just seeing that reminder makes me feel overwhelmed all over again.

Cashol glances up at me, and then shakes his head. "Oh no."

"What?"

"You have the hopper face again."

"Hopper face?" I sputter. "What's a hopper face?"

"The one you made just before you started weeping." He gives me a wary expression. "Are you going to weep again?"

"No....maybe." But I smile a little. "So what's the hopper face *look* like?"

Cashol looks up from the fire he's feeding small bits of fluff to. He squints at me, and then his mouth positively contorts as he mimics me, and it's so ridiculous and overblown that I burst into laughter.

"I do NOT look like that!"

"You do," he assures me, grinning. "I could not tell if you were going to sneeze or weep."

I laugh harder, because okay, maybe I do look like that. "You shouldn't be teasing me about that."

"Why not? I like your laughter far more than your tears." He leans in and blows on the fire, stoking the flames higher, and I watch his tail move back and forth with far too much interest. Since when do I find tails fascinating? Yet I can't seem to stop watching his. It's a bit like a cat's, but sometimes it flicks and curls in a way that no cat's ever could, and I'm utterly transfixed. Maybe I just need to get laid more if I'm obsessing over tails.

Of course, the one that's supposed to be sleeping with me won't, and that thought makes me gloomy all over again.

"I think that is good for the fire," Cashol announces. "We will stay here and warm up, and then return home later."

"Sure."

If he notices my lack of enthusiasm, he doesn't say

anything. Instead, he's quiet as he moves to the back of the cave and grabs his bag, pulling the dead hopper out and hiding it against his chest as he moves to the front of the cave to bury it in the snow—this place's version of frozen food. It's kinda sweet that he thinks I'm distressed over hoppers. It's just the straw that broke the camel's back, showing me that I'll never be able to swing it here.

He returns a few moments later, and then moves to my side, pulling at the laces of my sodden boots. "We will give these a chance to dry, too."

"Okay."

I remain still as he pulls my soaked boots off my feet, and my toes are pale white and cold, and I shiver, sticking them as close to the fire as I dare. I know the cootie will take care of any frostbite, but it's still unpleasant to think about. I glance over at Cashol, and he's taking his own boots off, so I guess I'm not the only one with wet feet. I watch, lost in thought, as he props a spear against a crevice in the cave wall and lowers the head of it to the top of the tripod over the fire, creating a clothes-line that he drapes with our wet leathers. "That's smart," I comment.

"I am full of smart things," he says cockily.

I know he's being like that just to make me smile, but it's working. "Full of something, all right."

He just grins back at me, all boyish enthusiasm, and then sits down next to me and immediately plops one ginormous foot into my lap.

I sputter in surprise. "What is this for?"

"You are going to rub my foot, and I am going to rub yours." Cashol nods at me, that playful expression on his face. "You like a foot rubbing, do you not?"

I'm not sure if he's asking about giving or receiving. I eye his enormous foot and then hesitantly put my hands on it. Am I weird if I find his feet incredibly attractive? Because having one right in front of me just emphasizes how perfect I find this particular body part of his. Not that all of him isn't incredibly appealing. How funny that a month ago I would have said that Cashol was probably the lowest on the totem pole of looks in the tribe, but now I can't see anyone but him. I love his big nose and wild grin. I love his long face and the way he looks slightly disheveled all the time, as if he's a whirlwind that's paused only for a moment. I love his big feet and his broad shoulders...

And I wish like hell he'd touch me again.

I rub my thumbs into the underside of his foot, trying not to fall back into that deep slide of anxiety that threatens to overwhelm me. It does no good to be sad about things. I just need to find a way to make myself indispensable. Then, everything will work itself out.

I eye the big foot in my lap, curling my hands around it. "Your feet aren't cold at all."

"Yours are like ice," he mutters, rubbing briskly. "It is like I am hugging frozen meat."

I giggle and slide my hands over his enormous foot. He'd at least be a size sixteen if we were back home, I think. Ginormous feet, and they match the rest of him. I run my fingers over his three large, strange toes and then rub the arch. "I guess I am lucky, then. I don't mind touching yours."

He groans when I hit a particular spot, eyes closing. "I think I am lucky, too." He's barely rubbing my own feet, but I don't mind, because he's holding them and his big hands are warm, and that's good enough. When I chuckle, Cashol glances over at me. "I am glad to hear you laugh again. I have missed hearing it."

I manage another smile, but I don't feel this one. "I haven't had much to laugh over, I guess."

"Why are you sad? Can you tell me?"

The knot returns to my throat, and I stare down at his perfect feet, wishing I was in the right frame of mind to appreciate getting to put my hands all over them. "I just...feel like I'm failing at all of this."

"All of what?"

"Living here. Killing things. Making fires. Being a good tribesmate. I worry..." I pause, and then push on. "I worry that I'm going to be a burden and people aren't going to want me here."

Cashol scoffs. "That is a silly fear."

"Doesn't feel silly to me." I shrug. "Why wouldn't the tribe decide I'm not worth it? You did."

He's silent.

16

MEGAN

In fact, he's silent for so long that I feel like an asshole for saying anything. For confronting what we've both been skirting around for the past two weeks. "I'm sorry," I finally say. "I know I'm not the mate you wanted, but I shouldn't have said that."

His hand squeezes on my foot and he looks at me with a curious expression. "Why would you think you are not the mate I wanted?"

"You're avoiding me. You don't want to sleep with me. Ever since we fulfilled resonance..." I shrug. "You act like you don't want anything to do with me."

"Meh-gan," he murmurs, voice soft. "You are exactly the mate I wanted. If I could tell my khui to choose one female, it would absolutely be you."

"I don't understand," I tell him with a shake of my head. "You go out hunting all day long—"

He gives me an odd look, one of his huge smiles on his face. "Meh-gan, hunting is a part of life. Of course I must go out."

"But did you have to go right after we resonated? Do you have to stay out so very late? And even when you come back, you don't spend time with me."

"You are always busy!" He gestures at my hands. "Every time I speak to you, you are working with others on a hide, or you are making a belt, or you have three things going at once. I do not want to bother you when you are getting so much work done—"

"I'm getting so much work done so no one will kick me out of the tribe!"

"No one is kicking you anywhere!"

My mouth twitches as I stare at him, and I can't decide if I want to laugh or cry at that ridiculous statement. He doesn't get it. He was born here and he has always fit in. No one would ever think of booting Cashol for not carrying his weight. "It's not just that," I point out. "You immediately made another bed for yourself, right after we resonated."

A flash of guilt shows on his expressive face. "I did not wish to disturb your sleep."

"We're mated. We're together. Forever. Why would you think that means I don't want sex? Why are you avoiding me?" Hot tears prick my eyes again.

He sighs, the sound heavy and defeated. "It is a long, complicated story."

"I have nowhere to go." I indicate our surroundings.

Cashol pauses, then adds, "It is a long, complicated story I have no wish to tell right now."

I shake my head at him. "I don't understand you. Or any of this. Is it some sort of ritual I don't know about? Is it that you can't have sex during certain times of the month? What?" I haven't heard anything of the sort, but a small part of me hopes it can all be explained away in some logical reason I haven't thought of.

"No ritual. It is just me." His expression is sad and somehow full of yearning.

"You mean it's me," I say bitterly. "You just don't want me." I shove his beautiful foot out of my lap and try to pull my own feet away. "Just tell the truth. Don't sugar-coat it or play games with me, all right? I'm so sick of all of this—"

He doesn't let go of my foot, his strong fingers locking around my ankle, and I kick at him again. And again, and then he captures my other foot. "Why are you convinced it is you?" he asks, even as he drags me forward on the furs, pulling me toward his now-crossed legs as if tugging me into his lap.

"Because no one ever wants me enough. There's a saying that if you meet one asshole all day, that guy is the asshole. If everyone you meet is an asshole, then you're the asshole. Well, no one ever wants to stay in a relationship with me, so I figure I'm the problem. I—" I twist as he tugs me even closer to him. "What are you doing?"

"I am going to kiss my asshole," he says, grinning.

That makes me break into a furious round of giggles. He tugs me into his lap, my legs spread over his hips, until I'm straddling him, and I press my fingers to his mouth. "Do me a favor and don't say that around the others. They're going to think it's a flexibility thing."

"A what?"

"Never mind. I'll tell you later." I slide my arm around his neck and look him in the eye, so sad. I love his long face with the big grin and the prominent nose. I want to kiss every inch of him. Why doesn't he want me back? "So...what are we doing? Really?"

"I am going to kiss you," Cashol says slowly, his gaze on my mouth. His hands slide up my backside, squeezing, and I can feel the rock-hard length of him in his loincloth, pressing against my core. "And then I am going to lay you down in these furs and lick your cunt until all your tears wash away."

Oh. Oh, that sounds rather delightful, even to my messed-up head. "You want to kiss me?"

"More than anything." He says it with an ache, as if he's waited forever to tell me that. He squeezes my ass, gazing at me fiercely. "My pretty Meh-gan. Will you let me?"

I nod. Of course I will. He's my mate, and I desperately need to feel connected to someone right now. Our night together was incredible, so kissing is no hardship. His mouth brushes over mine, ever so gentle, and I moan at the sensation, burying my fingers in his hair.

I didn't know how badly I needed this.

His mouth is exquisite, and when he dips his tongue against mine, I feel it all through my body. My cootie purrs a happy song, as if reminding me that Cashol has been its choice all along. My body responds to the kiss, to the slow, gentle sweep of his hands up and down my back, to the feel of his big frame against my smaller one. It's been the two longest weeks of my life since our last mating, and I've spent every moment of it doubting myself, doubting that what we had together was truly that good. That maybe it was just a figment of my imagination.

But when Cashol rolls our twined bodies forward and I rest on my back in the furs with him over me, I know it wasn't just the cootie. I feel it now, when his big hand skates down my belly. I quiver with need when he tugs at the waistband of my leggings and pulls them down my thighs. He lifts my ankle and kisses it once he tugs it free of my clothing, then kisses all the way up the inside of my thigh.

"Boy, you're not wasting any time," I breathe, watching him with utter fascination.

"I am not," he agrees. "Because I have been dreaming of this every night. I have hungered for your taste, longed for your scent..." He leans forward, tucking one leg over his shoulder, and spreads my thighs. He gazes down at my pussy, as if feasting his eyes, and with a low groan, lowers his head and drags his tongue over the seam of my folds.

I whimper, my fingers curling into the furs.

"You taste better than I remember," he murmurs, his breath hot against my skin. "I remembered the feel of this against my nose." And his fingers brush over my curls. "I remembered the way your third nipple felt when I sucked on it, and I—"

"W-wait, what?" Third nipple?

"This," he tells me, and his tongue traces around my clit in a way that makes my entire body jerk in response. I whimper, letting my thighs fall wider. "Tasting your third nipple."

"Clit," I breathe, trying to think straight. "It's called a clit."

"I do not care what it is called as long as it is on my tongue." He flicks it again, and then sucks powerfully, making me cry out. He says nothing else, returning to licking my clit with such enthusiasm that I forget everything but the feel of his mouth. He pushes a finger deep inside me and I arch with utter delight. God, he's good at this.

He makes a noise of pure appreciation as he pumps into me with his finger, his mouth locked on my clit. I don't last long—I'm in far too emotional a state and a release is exactly what I need. I let the sensations sweep over me, and when the orgasm erupts, I take it with a greedy whimper, enjoying every swipe of his tongue over my sensitized flesh.

Cashol lifts his head when I come down, and our eyes meet. I smile at him, breathless, and in this moment he might be the most beautiful man I've ever seen. "That went too fast," he says mournfully, kissing the inside of my thigh over and over again. "I barely got started."

"You act like we're done." I reach for him. "Come. I want you inside me."

He sits up on his elbows, and gives me a thoughtful look. "Not right now."

My happy, dazed release disappears, and I'm left with all those feelings of uncertainty. I draw my legs closed, trying to scoot away from him. "What do you mean, not right now?"

My big alien mate lets me sit up. He rolls onto his side, keeping a possessive hand on my knee, and his thumb brushes over my skin as he gazes up at me. "This was just for you, my Meh-gan. I will take my pleasure later."

"When we get back to the main cave?" Surely we have time for a quickie.

"No. Later than that."

"Er, how much later?" When he shrugs, I fight the urge to kick him. "What is going on with you, Cashol? How can you say you want me and then act like this?"

He stares down at his thumb as he brushes it over my thigh. "Because I do want you, Meh-gan. I want you more than anything. I have never wavered on that. But I was weak on the night of our resonance. I let myself get carried away and I did not do what was best for my mate."

Best for his mate? "And what the heck is that?"

"Waiting," he says simply. "I want to wait until you are ready."

"I'm ready right now," I snap. "Didn't I just tell you I wanted to have sex?"

"But do you want it because you can think of nothing but Cashol and his strong limbs? That you are beside yourself with desire? Or do you want it because you feel it will secure your place in the tribe better because I have given you my heart?"

That makes me stop. For all that Cashol is a laughing tease, sometimes he sees to the heart of the matter. Do I really want him, or do I just want to have sex because it's expected of resonance mates and I want so desperately to please everyone? "I...I don't know," I whisper. "I'm kind of ashamed I don't know."

"I overheard you speaking to Jo-see," he confesses. "She asked if you were happy and you said you were not sure."

I did? I don't remember that. I shrug, opening my mouth to protest. I'm sure I say lots of things off the cuff. Sometimes I say what people expect to hear, because no one wants to know what I'm really thinking. "I'm not sure I know if I can be happy here," I admit to him. "I feel lost."

"I lost my heart to you the first time I saw you," Cashol admits to me. "You did not learn my name for many nights after that, but it did not matter. You have always held it in your hands." He strokes my thigh, and I have to admit, that feels pretty good. Not quite as good as oral, but right now I just like being touched. I didn't know how much I craved it, actually. "But I want a mate who smiles at me with her eyes and tells me her thoughts, not a mate who tells me that she is fine and her eyes are full of worry."

Busted. Has anyone ever known me so well? "I'm just... trying to cope."

"I know. I am not judging you. But I am also not pressuring you." He leans in and kisses my knee, as if he can't stand to not touch me, just a little. "I want to give you time. On the day you wake up and think, I cannot go another step without Cashol's great cock inside me, I will be happily waiting for you."

I chuckle at his words, and then a new worry hits me. "I... what if it takes a while?"

"I am not a patient hunter, but I am trying." He smiles at me. "The prey this time is worth an extended hunt."

I lift my foot and use it to gently push his shoulder. "Maybe you don't call it a hunt."

His smile broadens and he grabs my foot, kissing it and sending a flare of heat through my body. "What would you call it?"

"I have no idea. When I think of it, I'll let you know." It's not exactly a wooing. It's more like...a waiting. I hesitate. "So you and me...where are we?"

He glances around. "We are in a hunter cave."

I shove him with my foot again, and he catches it, chuckling, and nips at my big toe. "I'm serious," I tell him, getting all breathless again. He's dangerous with that mouth, and I have far too much of a thing for feet. "You and I...where do we go from here?"

"I wait for you to be ready to love me," Cashol says, nibbling on my toe. He really is the most distracting man.

"Does this mean you're going to keep sleeping apart from me? Because...I don't like it. It hurts my feelings." Confessing this makes me feel like the biggest baby in the world. I feel like I'm whining, and that he's going to tell me I'm clingy and needy like guys have in the past.

But Cashol just considers this. "I did not realize it would hurt your feelings."

"How can it not?"

He gives me a sheepish look. "I am new to being mated. You are my first mate in all ways. There is much I do not know."

Okay, fine, I'll give him that. "Why would you think I wouldn't want to sleep with you, though? Even as...friends?" God, it feels weird to say that.

"Because it is easier for me if we do not sleep together," he admits. "If I touch you, I will want you, and I do not want to pressure you. I want you to come to me when you are ready."

Oh. That makes sense, really. "I guess we can keep sleeping apart, then. I just wish you would have told me the reasoning behind it."

"I wish you would have told me you were afraid of being rejected by the tribe. I would have told you how foolish that is. Look at Drenol and the elders. They can barely leave their caves on days that their bones ache. I do not think Eklan has left the cave in many turns of the seasons. Yet no one would dream of casting them out."

"Yes, but they're your people. It's different."

"How is it different? You are my people."

"No, I'm a human. An outsider. I don't know how to do anything."

He sits up and reaches for my hands, clasping them in his. "If this worries you, then I will teach you all that I know. If you wish to make fire, I will show you. If you wish to hunt fish with nets, I will show you. If you wish to make sinew out of dvisti intestine, I will show you. Anything and everything I know, I will share it." He takes my hands and lifts them to his mouth. "Just do not cry."

Maybe it's the orgasm, or maybe it's the smile on his face (or the conversation we just had) but I feel a lot better about things now. "I'm glad we talked."

"I am glad we did a great many things," Cashol says, grinning wickedly. "Talking among them."

I hesitate, because I wonder if I should offer him a blow job. Go down on him to ease his aches. I want to do that because... because it's expected of a woman? Because we're not supposed to receive and not give?

Man, he's right. How often do I do things because I expect that's what people want from me? Cashol just wants me to be me.

That might be harder than I realize.

17

CASHOL

We return to the cave that night, and even though it is dark by the time we make it back to our cave and Meh-gan is shivering from the cold, I decide it has been a good day. We have talked through some of our problems, and Meh-gan's smile is lighter. She holds my hand as we return, and her laughter is bright and bubbling as we trek back.

My tongue still has the memory of her taste on it.

So yes, all in all, a very good day.

I offer to turn the hopper over to Sevvah, but Meh-gan has recovered from her earlier distress. "Maybe I can't kill things, but I can at least clean and cook," she offers to me. "And there's no sense in wasting a perfectly good hopper."

Truly, she is stronger than she thinks. Not all who contribute to the tribe hunt. It is not necessary as long as we have plenty of hunters to bring in enough for everyone. And with me as her mate, Meh-gan needs to never hunt for herself.

But I hold those words back, because Meh-gan wants to learn to be self-sufficient, so I will show her other things she can do.

Our cave is cold from the fire being out all day, so I show Meh-gan how I build a fire. I take my time to demonstrate each step, trying not to notice just how near she leans, or how good she smells. I pay attention to the fire itself, not the curve of her pretty mouth or the teat that presses up against my arm as she leans in to see.

Slow, I remind myself. We are going slow.

This afternoon was a wonderful treat, but if Meh-gan does not wish for me to touch her again, I must honor her wishes. As Vektal said, she needs time, and today's crying storm proves that she is upset and scared, despite the smiles she wears on her face. The memory of her anguish makes my cock deflate, and I am able to concentrate on the task at hand. "Tomorrow," I tell her, "you will practice more with the fire."

Her broad smile, bright and reaching her eyes, is all of the thanks I need.

As I hang her fur wraps in the cave to dry off, Meh-gan skins the hopper and cuts the meat into strips. She is getting much better at that, I realize, and it reminds me of just how much she has pushed herself since she and the other females arrived. My mate works until she is falling asleep, and that cannot help but add to her stress. It will make her tired—not just in the body, but in the mind.

It is a good thing she has me to distract her.

Once the furs are hung, I watch as she cleans her hands in a bowl of icy water. I slide in next to her by the fire, tempted to grab one of her cold feet and rub it again, when she gestures at the food spread out on a bone platter.

"You are not going to burn it?" I ask her.

Meh-gan's mouth twitches with amusement. "It's called 'cooking' and no, I'm not. Raw isn't too bad. I'm getting more and more used to it."

I wonder if this is another thing that she is determined to do in order to be more like the rest of the sa-khui tribe. I do not say so. Instead, I pick up the platter and hold out a cube of meat. "Eat."

Her brows draw together and she laughs. "What, you're going to feed me?"

"Yes, I am."

She laughs, shaking her head as if this is the silliest thing ever. I do not care—I like the idea of feeding my mate and I want to do so. I hold the bit of meat out to her and wait, and with another little laugh, she leans forward and takes the morsel into her mouth. Her lips brush over my fingers, and then she leans back, chewing, a smile on her face as her fingertips go to her mouth.

All the blood in my body surges to my cock. Perhaps I should not be feeding her, because now I am thinking about her mouth on my cock, her mouth on my skin, and the night of our resonance when we mated so many times that I lost count. I watch her, hungry with need, as she takes a sip of water from her waterskin and then settles in, moving a little closer to me. "It's good. Aren't you going to eat?"

"After you," I manage, and I am relieved that I sound normal enough. I offer her another bite, hoping for her lips to touch my fingertips again and sad when they do not.

We talk a little about the weather, and of silly nothings, and she eats from my fingertips, and I am entranced by how delicate she is, how fragile. Why did I take her hunting? Leezh goes with Raahosh, but most of the females stay near the cave, and I can see why. It was difficult for her to keep up with me through the snow, her short legs and small feet unable to power through as I do. When I warmed her feet, they felt like ice, and I made her cry because she felt she was unable to keep up. That she was disappointing me.

I am ashamed that I made her feel as if she was not worthwhile. Nothing has made me happier than Meh-gan's smiles.

Well, perhaps her touch.

"I'm sorry about earlier," she mentions quietly.

I lick the blood off my fingertips, and I see Meh-gan's gaze follow my mouth. "Sorry about what?"

"About crying. Having a nervous breakdown. All that." She manages a wobbly smile. "It wasn't the hunting or you or anything. It was just...everything has been getting to me, I think."

"I said nothing."

"No, but you got quiet, and I could tell what you were thinking. You have a super-obvious face." She smiles to take the sting out of her words. "I bet you're a terrible liar."

"I am not."

"See, right there, you just proved it." She grabs a piece of meat from the tray and holds it up to my mouth, and my heart warms. I take the bit, letting my teeth brush against her fingertips, and she lets out a little squeal of delight when I do. "Don't bite me!"

"I thought you liked it when I bit you."

Meh-gan laughs, and as I chew, she puts her hand to my cheeks and makes a silly face. "Are you flirting with me? You bad boy. I'm trying to have a moment with you."

"I like this moment," I tell her, smiling even as I chew. "I like this moment a lot."

Her laughter dies and she gives me a shy smile. "I do, too."

WE SPEND THE REST OF THE EVENING JUST TALKING AT OUR FIRE. Meh-gan wraps up in her furs and tells me stories of her world that seem ridiculous. How people would keep animals as "pets" and let them live with them, and even sleep under the furs with them. She had something called a "dogh" once and tells me she was a "hors-gurl" when she was little. She tells me the food in their world comes from small, square containers in a cave, or that she would walk up to a cave and people would hand her a meal in exchange for valuable round disks she calls "mah-nee."

It sounds ridiculous. Why would anyone hunt all day for food and then hand it over to a stranger for disks? But she promises it is so, so I must believe her.

Meh-gan keeps her fingers busy, weaving one of her belts as she talks, but her movements are slower tonight, as if all of her is tired. Her eyelids grow heavy and she yawns through our conversation until I take the leatherwork from her and shake my head. "You are tired. Go to sleep."

"I...wanted to get...finished tonight..." she protests, trying to take it from my hands.

"It will be there tomorrow." I put it aside. "Go to sleep. There is no point in tiring yourself over a project."

"Supposed to start a new one...tomorrow..." Meh-gan yawns again and gives up. She retreats to the bed and curls up in the furs. "You coming?"

"I will sleep over here," I say, gesturing at my own pitiful nest of furs. "It will be easier."

She makes a face at my decision, but says nothing else, and within moments, she is asleep. I watch her sleep for a while, poking at the fire, and protective feelings for Meh-gan overwhelm me.

I had no idea she was trying to be so strong. That she was so determined to be thought of as useful that she was fretting over it. That is why she cried—it wasn't the hopper but her frustration with her own inability to be what she thinks I need her to be.

She does not understand. All I need her to be is Meh-gan. My beautiful Meh-gan with the sharp, sly tongue who laughs at me when I push too hard and looks at me with a welcome smile. I understand her fears, though. Did I not feel alone when my father died and I realized I had no one left? No family cave to return to? It was not until I moved in with the other hunters that I felt as if I belonged again.

All I can do is make Meh-gan feel welcome and safe. She must learn the rest on her own.

I add the leftover bits of meat to a drying rack and then settle into my furs to sleep, my thoughts on my troubled mate and how I can make her smile. Hunting is not the way. I need to find things around the cave that will make her feel useful and happy.

A whimper stirs me before I can drift to sleep.

I sit up, immediately looking over at my mate.

Meh-gan tosses and turns in her sleep, a frown on her face. She whimpers again, curling into a tight ball. "No," she mutters. "No. No."

"Meh-gan," I whisper. "You are dreaming."

"No," she says again, and the sound is heartbroken. "Oh, no—"

I reach over and touch her shoulder.

Meh-gan gasps and jerks awake, clutching at my arm. Her eyes are wide with fear and she is sweating. She gulps, blinking rapidly, and I can tell she is terrified.

"It was a dream," I tell her. "Just a dream."

Her face crumples. "Right. Sure. A dream."

"A bad one?" I ask.

"Wasn't good." Her eyes fill with tears and she sniffs, then takes a deep, shuddery breath. "It was about the aliens."

The ones that stole her. I touch her cheek. "You are safe from them. I will not let anyone hurt you."

"Thank you," she whispers, and when I pull away, her hands linger on my arm, as if she does not wish to let me go. "Sorry to wake you up."

"You must truly stop apologizing."

"I will. Someday." She manages a weak smile and then tugs the blankets closer to her. She looks small and very alone in the furs, and I can tell she is unsettled by her dream.

Perhaps I will regret this decision in the morning, but I do not have the heart to be cruel now. "Would you like to come and sleep beside me?"

She hesitates. "Is it going to bother you?"

"No." Her fear bothers me more.

Meh-gan gives me a brilliant, shy smile, and then grabs her blankets and drags them over to my nest. I add her furs to the warm pile and then lift one corner, indicating she should crawl in next to me. She does, and immediately tucks herself against me, her back to my front, her bottom fitting perfectly against my cock. She takes my arm and wraps it around her waist, as if she needs desperately to be held, and I slide my other around her, too, cradling her against me.

She lets out a little sigh that sounds so very content.

I hold her close, breathing in her scent, and notice that she settles in right away. Her eyes close and she falls asleep before I can even tease her about how cold her feet are as she presses them against my bare legs.

My cock does ache with her nearness, but not as much as my heart. Perhaps this is another way I am going about things all wrong. Perhaps Meh-gan needs to be held a lot more. Perhaps two nests of furs is a terrible idea.

I hold her closer against me, my tail wrapping around her ankle, and drift off to sleep, dreaming of Meh-gan handing me food in exchange for mah-nee disks.

18

MEGAN

I wake up with my nose pressed against Cashol's warm, broad chest, and my feet tucked between his thighs, his tail locked around one ankle. I'm cramped and his weight is resting on one of my hands, but I still feel more refreshed after sleeping next to him than I have in weeks. I sit up slowly, uncurling myself from our heap of furs and trying not to wake him up. It's early, judging by the sounds in the main cave, and that means I can get a jump start on the day. I need more leather cords for my belts, so that means cutting leather strips and tying them together, and that means digging through storage and—

Cashol makes a soft sound and drags me back into bed next to him. "Come back."

"I should get up," I protest, smiling as he wraps his big body around me, trapping me against his chest. He's enormous, this man, and he makes me feel positively puny next to him.

"But why?" He holds me against him and I wish he would

kiss my neck, or rub that morning wood he's sporting against my backside, but he doesn't. He just cuddles me.

"Because there's a lot to get done." My mind is on fire with belts, really. Cashol brought a pack with him yesterday, but he mostly used it like I would a purse—it held knives, and cords, and he constantly pulled it out looking for items. I think I can make him a belt and sew small pouches on it to organize his things, and perhaps another belt to cross over his shoulder. They would need additional loops for things like rope, but I bet I can make it work and make it easier to access.

And I'll get started...just as soon as Cashol lets me go.

He only snuggles me closer to his chest.

"The fire's out," I cajole. "Don't you want me to practice my fire-making skills?"

He groans and opens one eye to squint at me. "Why did I mate to a female who is up first thing in the morning?"

"You're just lucky," I tease, prying his tail off my ankle. "And you know I'm right."

Cashol sits up as I get out of bed and head for the cave's version of a bathroom. I wash up afterward, shivering at the cold water, and then sit down by the fire to make it myself. Normally we stir the coals, leaving a large chunk of fuel burning in the center so it won't be completely dead by morning, or I grab a coal from the main fire and transport it to my hearth using a hollowed out animal horn. Today, though, I want to learn. Cashol gets dressed, yawning as he sits beside me, and then walks me through how to make a fire. I use the bow he hands me, but try as I might, I can't get enough power going to produce a spark.

"Give it time," he tells me as he sees my frustration. "No one learns in a day." He presses a kiss to the top of my head. "I must go and check my trap lines, but I will return quickly and then we will spend the rest of the day together, yes?"

"If you want to."

"Oh, I want to." He grins at me. "We are going to have a day of laziness."

Yeah, sure.

⁜

To my surprise, Cashol returns within a few hours. It's barely even time for the midday meal to be prepped when he strolls back in with several fat carcasses and hands them off to the elders to go in the day's stew.

"You're back," I say with surprise as he comes over to my side. I'm sitting not too far away from the main fire, only half-listening in on the conversation as Kemli and Sevvah discuss the best way to dry a certain type of needle-leaf. I have the pieces for Cashol's new belt spread out in front of me, and I pause in my work when he presses a happy kiss atop my head. "Why are you back so fast?"

"It is because he has a pretty mate to return to," Kemli teases us, turning to give Cashol a knowing look. "It makes his feet speed over the snow."

Cashol just leans in close and whispers in my ear. "I move faster by myself."

"Because you didn't have to drag me along?" I feel guilty that I made the effort so much harder for him yesterday, and then made it even worse by crying.

He shakes his head, his hair tickling my face as he leans over me. "Because I ran most of the way."

I snort-giggle with amusement as he gives me a cheeky look.

Cashol plucks the leather strips out of my hands and ignores the protest I make. "You have been working too hard. For the rest of the afternoon, it shall be a day of laziness."

"Oh, I don't know..." I glance over at the women, wondering if we're going to be judged. Sevvah just rolls her eyes at Cashol and goes back to talking to Kemli. Neither one looks all that concerned with the thought of me having a "day of laziness."

"Are you sure?"

"I am sure," Cashol says, gathering up the leather strips and loops and tossing them into a pile. "I am going to relax, and you are going to keep me company." He gestures at the bathing pool in the center of the cavern. "And we are going to start in there."

"Mmmhmm." As he grabs the pile of leather pieces, several of them drop to the ground. I scoop them up and follow after him as he heads to our cave. "It sounds to me like someone's making excuses so I'll wash his back for him."

"And my front," he adds cheerfully.

I laugh. "Can't do just one side, I guess. I'd hate for your dirt to be uneven."

"It is true. I am very, very dirty." Cashol gives me an arch look that makes me burst into a fit of giggles. It's clear he's just talking about general dirt, and I'm taking it to a filthy, sexual place, but it's so damn funny to hear. He just makes me laugh, and I love it. Being around him makes my heart feel so much lighter, and I already feel better. I spare one last glance at the elders to see if they're judging us, but no one seems to have noticed. Maybe they really don't care. Maybe I can just relax and not worry about fitting in.

We drop our things off back to our cave, and I'm a little surprised when Cashol immediately strips and saunters out to the bathing pool, buck-ass naked. He is *clearly* not shy. I undress but keep a fur wrapped around me as I head toward the bathing pool, and drop it at the side. I'm not entirely used to the nudity. Not quite yet.

Nora and Josie are already bathing, and I smile awkwardly at them as my big, naked mate hops into the pool and accidentally splashes them. "Hey, watch it," Nora says. "I'm trying not to get my hair wet." Her highlights are growing out, revealing ash-brown roots, and she's got a carved stick poked through a bun of hair to keep it dry. "So how's the newlyweds?"

"Great," I say, and poke Cashol in the side before he can contradict me. I beam at both of them. "Where's Dagesh today?"

Nora gives a great, gusty sigh and sinks lower into the water. "Hunting with Harrec and Warrek. He won't be back for a week or so. They're replenishing one of the caches near the Ancestors' Cave." She makes a moue of displeasure. "I miss him already."

Cashol makes an unhappy sound. "They left already? And took Warrek with them?"

"Yeah, Dagesh figured that you wouldn't be up for leaving your mate for so long just yet." She shrugs. "It's no big deal. I think Warrek was thrilled to be invited."

"And Farli's thrilled that she doesn't have to have lessons while he's gone." Josie grins. "She's supposed to join us but she went to the storage cave for more soap-berries and hasn't come back yet."

I glance over at Cashol, and he's got a troubled look on his face. It's clear that not going on the hunt is bothering him, and I fight down a surge of panic. I'm glad he didn't go. The thought of him leaving my side for that long makes me utterly panicky. I can deal with a few hours, but a week? I'm not ready. Before Cashol can speak up, I grab him by the shoulders and push down, trying to dunk him in the deep pool. He goes under, the water bubbling with his breath, and Josie erupts into a fit of laughter.

A moment later, his tail locks around my foot, and before I can celebrate my "win," I'm pulled under, too. Sputtering, I find my way back to the surface and Cashol pulls me into his arms, nipping at my jaw. "That was naughty of you."

I grab his chin and slide my arm around his shoulders, floating next to him in the water. "I don't want you volunteering to go on a long hunt," I whisper, keeping my voice low enough so the others don't hear. "You have to stay with me."

He nods, sensing my unease. "I will not leave your side, do not worry."

Relieved, I sink into his arms. "Maybe you don't dunk me, either."

"Maybe you do not dunk me," he counters.

"Oh my god, enough with the flirting," Nora says, splashing a small wave over at us. "You're making me miss my man."

"Sorry." The water's like a hot tub, and I can blame my blush on that, I hope. I glance over at Josie and she's smiling at us, but there's a wistful expression on her face. I know how it feels to want this so badly. There's not many left that haven't resonated, and it's hard to not feel like a reject when there's so many single guys and your khui doesn't speak up. I make a mental note to try and spend some time with my friend tomorrow, so she feels included.

"Look what I found!" Farli comes racing out of one of the storage caves, a basketball-sized not-potato in her skinny arms. She's completely naked, too, her long hair pulled back into twin braids that run alongside her curving horns. "Look!"

"Uh, we're not washing with that, baby girl," Nora comments. "That's a vegetable."

"Not that, ding-dong," Josie says, and points. "It's got a big bite taken out of it."

Farli nods at Josie, turning the root so we can all see. Sure enough, the white meat of the not-potato root is exposed, and it looks as if a big chunk was gnawed out of it.

"Yuck." Nora wrinkles her nose.

"Did someone take a bite and put it back?" Farli asks, juggling it in her arms.

I laugh at the suggestion. "Oh sure."

The girl turns wide eyes to me. "Really?"

"Oh yeah, it was me. I tasted that one and decided it was no good, and put it back. You have to taste all of the roots to decide which ones are the best," I tease. "I thought everyone knew that."

Nora shakes her head at me, laughing, as Farli's eyes grow even wider.

Josie moves to the lip of the pool, gesturing at Farli. "You should probably throw that out. No one's going to want to eat it."

Farli looks over at me uncertainly.

"I'm teasing," I say, feeling a little bad at the joke. "I don't even like not-potato when it's raw."

"Did you find berries?" Josie asks Farli.

"I did!" She dumps the chewed-on root by the pool and then races back to the caves again. "Be right back!"

Josie sighs, grinning. "She's just the cutest kid."

"Bah. You are both close to the same age," Cashol says, pulling me into his lap and wrapping his arms around my waist.

"We are not!" Josie says, outraged. She splashes toward us. "At least I'm not the one eating all the damn food in storage."

"My mate does have an uncontrollable appetite," Cashol says solemnly. "I must hunt and hunt to feed her belly."

"Oh, are we talking about food?" Nora teases, the minx. "I thought we were going on about different insatiable appetites."

Josie immediately puts her fingers in her ears. "La la la, I can't hear you."

Nora cackles with delight, and I sink lower into the water, trying to hide my laughter. Nora's fun. She makes no bones about who she is. She absolutely hated being here until she took one look at Dagesh, and then she decided she loved this place. Every knows the two of them are very enthusiastic and noisy in the furs. Everyone. And Nora doesn't care. She's happy and she's in love, and she doesn't give a fig what anyone else thinks.

God, I wish I was like her. I wish I didn't have this gnawing fear in my belly that I'm not going to be enough for any of these people.

Farli returns with a large soap-berry pouch and sets it down on the ledge between Nora and Josie, and then gets into the water next to them. Cashol holds onto me, dragging me through the water over to the berries and grabs a handful.

"What are you doing?" I ask him.

"I am going to wash my mate," he says proudly.

"Oh my god, that's so cute," Josie squeals. "I'm so happy for you guys." She says it to both of us, but she looks at me.

If only she knew how fucked up we are. But then again...are we? Because Cashol's been plenty flirty since we had that talk in the hunter cave yesterday. He went down on me and made me come, and wanted nothing in return except to hold me. I slept so good last night, snuggled in his arms. And today he's back from hunting early so he can lounge in the pool with me and wash my hair. I have to admit, I'm eating up all the attention I'm being showered with. I know I'm a needy sort in a relationship, but I've never had anyone feed my neediness. I've never had anyone be as into me as I am to them.

I don't want to get my hopes up with Cashol.

But my new mate cheerfully smashes berries onto my "flat, hornless head" and then leans in to nip at my ear, and I think about what he said.

When you are ready, I will be here.

No one's ever been there for me before...but I'm starting to believe him.

19

MEGAN

We spend a lazy few hours soaking in the pool, chatting with Farli and Josie and Nora, and talking about nothing in particular. Others come and go, and my fingers prune up and all the heat makes me sleepy, so we retreat back to our cave for an afternoon nap, of all things.

I don't think I've napped in the afternoon since I was a child, but Cashol lies down in the furs and indicates I should join him, and I jump right in next to him. His wet hair sticks to everything, and so does mine, and he tickles my sides...and then goes down on me again, giving me a hard, fast orgasm that makes me utterly breathless and saps the last of my strength.

So I nap, content and happy.

When I wake up, Cashol rubs a hand up and down my back. "You slept well."

"I did, didn't I?" I freely admit that sleeping next to him helps my too-active mind ease a little. Just having that human contact—or alien-human contact—makes me relax. I roll onto my back and stretch. "I should probably quit lazing about, though."

"No," he says, and sits up. "Now it is time."

"Time for what?" He's got a playful look on his face that makes me squint.

"Time for you to enjoy Cashol's rubbing cave."

I chuckle. "Rubbing cave, huh?"

He takes one of my feet in his hands. "I know you are fond of touching feet."

Touching feet. That's one way of putting it. More like I'm obsessed with touching his feet, not mine, but I'll take a foot rub. "So there's a special rubbing cave just set up for me, huh?"

"If there are caves where they hand you food, there is surely a rubbing cave." He works his fingers over my feet, kneading, and I have to admit, it does feel pretty good. I sigh happily and relax as he massages my toes and works his way down to my heel. "I had a good day today," he tells me.

"I did, too." Today is one of the happiest days I've had since I arrived here.

"I think we should have more days like today." When I open my eyes to look at him, he continues. "I will finish my trap lines early and then you and I will spend the day together."

"Doing what?"

Cashol shrugs. "We will go for walks. I will teach you how to do things. Do you fish?"

"No."

"Then we will learn that. And we can gather tea. And the roots you humans are so fond of."

"Is anyone going to get mad?"

"Why would they get mad? We will be providing for ourselves. No one will need to provide for us." He continues to rub my feet. "And I bring in enough with my traps that I can also provide extra meat for the tribe. But you are my first priority."

He's sweet. I have to admit that the idea of spending all this time with him makes me happy. "What if you get tired of being around me?"

He lets out a derisive snort. "I do not think that is possible."

Oh, it's possible. He can just ask all my ex-boyfriends back on Earth. But I suppose there's only one way to find out if we're going to get this right, and that's to spend time together. Lots of it. And learning how to fish and collecting roots is a good idea. I can work on my leather projects in the morning and help cook with either the morning meal or at lunch, and then head off with Cashol in the afternoon to do our own thing.

Getting away from the cave on the regular might be a good idea. Every moment that I spend here, I feel like I need to be focused on a task so they can see just how good of a worker I can be. "If you're sure it won't be a problem."

"I am sure." He rubs my foot harder. "And I think you need new boots."

"I do? Why?"

"Because your toes are always cold." He shakes his head.

I pull my foot free from his grip and poke him with one "cold" toe. "I don't know if you've noticed, but this is an ice planet."

"I do not know if *you* have noticed," he counters, "but your toes are cold when you press them against me at night."

My laughter dies in my throat. "I'm sorry. I'll sleep alone."

"No, you will not." He moves forward and lies down in the furs next to me, then tugs me into his arms. "I have not been very smart with all of this." Cashol slides his hands over my skin, pulling me against him until I'm practically plastered against his front. "I have decided that you are sleeping in the furs with me every night from now on."

"But what if I make certain parts of you ache?"

"Ah, but it is the best ache," he jokes. "And I do not regret it at all."

FOR THE NEXT THREE WEEKS, LIFE FEELS LIKE A DREAM. SURE, there's hard work involved, but I'm so happy. I can't stop smiling from sun-up to sun-down. We fall into a fairly easy pattern of daily work. I wake up early and sit by the fire, helping out with the cooking and working on Cashol's pouch-belts. They're a bit more involved than I initially thought, and I end up pulling the woven leather apart at least twice before I'm happy with how it's progressing. I also make simpler belts for Maylak and Eklan, both of whom admire my handiwork and I'm thrilled to make the gifts for them. In exchange, Maylak gives me a pouch of an herbal tea that helps with nausea—probably for the morning sickness I'm sure to have in the future—and Eklan makes me a few fishing lures out of tufts of meaty-looking fur bits attached to deadly hooks.

Once the twin suns are high in the sky, I start looking for Cashol's return. He always comes back at around the same time, usually with a fresh kill from his traps. After the kill is handed out or cleaned up for us to eat later, we spend the afternoon together.

Some afternoons, we go fishing, and I admit, I'm better at it than Cashol is. He isn't a great fisherman because he's impatient. He'll sit for a while by the water's edge, watching the lure dance along beneath the surface, but then he'll grow restless. He'll pick leaves by the shore and ask me to identify them. He'll see hopper tracks in the snow and want to chase them down. He'll go farther upstream and look for "things to spear."

The man just can't sit still and fish.

Me, I don't mind it. Fishing means sitting in one spot and teasing the line so the lure bobs and jerks and looks like a small, shrimplike creature that the fish love to eat. Eventually, it turns into a game to see if I can catch something before Cashol gets restless and races away again. In a way, it's kind of amusing

—my sa-khui mate is good at everything he puts his mind to, usually. He's good at hunting. He's fast on his feet. He's likeable. He's strong. He's great at kissing. Even better at going down on me.

Yet the man cannot sit still to save his life.

There are tracking lessons. Not because Cashol expects me to go and hunt something down, but so I can recognize which tracks are made from hunters coming and going, which tracks are wildlife, and which tracks are dangerous and should be avoided. One day we see metlak tracks far too close to our usual fishing spot, and so after that, we stay closer to the cave for lessons.

I eventually learn how to make a fire. I'm not fast at it, but given enough time and determination, I can now use the bow and spindle until I can get a spark. The day that I do, I feel a sense of utter elation and accomplishment, and Cashol's beaming grin tells me how proud he is of me, too.

There are berry picking runs, where we snag the tiny soap-berries from the bushes, or sometimes a sour-tasting, bitter green berry that grows on a piney-looking bush. Those berries are mostly used for the sticky sap they provide that acts as a good sealant. I'm told that the elders used to boil them down and mix them with another type of leaf to make a very pungent drink, but no one in the current generation likes the stuff. I also learn how to identify which plants are decent eating, which plants are poisonous, and which leaves are added to sah-sah to make the fermented drink so tasty.

Most nights end up with us by the fire, talking about nothing in particular. It's nice to just sit down and talk about the day, and most of the time, it leads to Cashol rubbing my feet...or me rubbing his feet. Of course, every time I rub his feet, I get turned on. There's just something about those enormous, perfect toes and his big heel and the feel of his strong foot against my fingers and I swear I'm squirming by the time five minutes have passed.

Cashol figures this out quickly and sticks his foot in my lap the moment we get back to the cave one night, and before we've even got the fire going, I'm on my back in the furs with his mouth between my thighs, and it's so good that I have to muffle my cries with the furs as he licks every sopping wet inch of me.

It's incredible. Every night, without fail, he goes down on me until I come—sometimes more than once—and then he holds me afterward. He never wants more than that, never wants me to reach for his cock and give him pleasure, too, though I know he's aching. He just wants it to be about me.

He tells me he'll wait for me to be ready.

And I want to be. He makes me so happy on days like this that I almost forget my worries. I'm not sure what I'm waiting for. Maybe I'm waiting for him to break, or for the universe to give me a sign.

Maybe I'm just enjoying what I have right now and not changing a thing, because I worry it won't last.

20

MEGAN

Two days later, it all falls apart. I knew it would. I'm sitting near the main fire, working on Cashol's belts again. I sit with Josie, talking about nothing in particular, and my seat is at the perfect angle so I can watch the front of the cave for Cashol's return. He promised to take me fishing today, and I'm looking forward to going out.

"Hmm." Kemli tastes the stew over the fire and then shakes her head. "It needs something. There are spices in the storage cave, Jo-see. Go and get them for me."

Farli jumps to her feet, scattering the strands of the net she was working on with Warrek and Eklan. "I'll get them!"

"No, you stir this, if you must help," Kemli says, handing her the ladle. "I need to cut some more meat."

Farli takes the ladle with a pout.

"Be right back." Josie smiles at me, bounces up, and then trots into the storage cave.

I go back to twisting my leather cords, trying to make an

elongated loop in the rest of the pattern so Cashol can hook things to his belt. The leather isn't playing nice—or it's not quite working out how I had it in my head, and I'm so distracted with trying to get it to braid just right that I don't notice how long it's taking Josie to return.

"Um, can you come here, Kemli?" Josie asks a little while later.

"Can you not find it?" Kemli puts down her knife, a little frown on her face. "It should be in one of the baskets at the front."

"That's not the problem." Josie gives me an uneasy look and I feel sick to my stomach. Why did she look at me specifically?

Farli stirs the stew with gusto, chattering. "Did you go and take bites out of everything while we were not looking, Meh-gan?" She giggles.

"Why would Meh-gan do that?" Eklan asks, his voice dry and raspy with age. He smiles at me, as if to say how silly Farli is being.

"Because pregnant females eat everything," Farli declares. "She is carrying after resonance, yes? And Meh-gan said she likes to taste the roots first. She puts them back if she does not like them."

Everyone turns to look at me.

"I-I was joking," I stammer. "Seriously. I would never."

I still might not feel as if I fit in a hundred percent, but I know there are certain things that the sa-khui take very seriously, and one of them is food. You eat everything that is handed to you, and it doesn't matter if you don't like the taste. Food isn't meant to be wasted, because the gathering and preserving of it for so many people is a monumental task. Even when I'm not keen on what's in the stew, I eat every bite, mindful of how much work went into it.

Kemli comes out of the storage cave a few moments later, with two not-potatoes in her arms, and Josie has one, too.

"Where is the chief?" Her face is taut with...anger? Irritation? "Where is Vektal?"

My stomach clenches again.

Georgie comes out of the cave she shares with Vektal, her brows furrowed. "Vektal's out hunting. He won't be back until late. What is it?"

Kemli purses her lips and holds one of the not-potatoes out. Sure enough, it's been gouged all over, as if someone took big, ugly bites out of it and put it back. The rest of the vegetable has discolored, and I know it's no good. You can't leave not-potato uncooked once you peel it or it turns bitter and rubbery.

"Someone has chewed on these," Kemli declares. "They are wasting food. All of the roots in storage look like this."

"But why would someone bite them and put them back?"

Farli looks at me curiously.

I jump to my feet, my heart pounding. "I swear, it wasn't me! I wouldn't do that!"

"No one said it was you, Megan," Georgie begins. "Let's all calm down."

"But why would you say such a thing?" Warrek asks, a curious note in his voice.

"It was a joke." I didn't think anyone was really going to go in and bite all the roots and make them rot. Why would I? It never occurred to me.

Kemli just shakes her head. "Someone bit these and now our food is ruined."

I jerk to my feet and gather the project I'm working on.

"Megan, calm down. Really. No one thinks you did it," Georgie says. "Really. It's okay."

But it's not okay. I feel as if Warrek and his father are judging me. That Kemli is looking at me with accusing eyes. That even Georgie isn't saying what she could to have my back. It's because they're all just looking for an excuse to get rid of dead weight around here...and the dead weight is me.

I should have known I can't be happy here. Something always happens to ruin my happiness. First they took my home from me, and then they took my baby. Now I feel as if I'm losing my new home and it hurts so badly that I can't breathe.

Because it means I'm going to lose Cashol, too. Of course he'd choose the tribe over me. Who wouldn't? They don't cling to him and tell him not to go hunt, and he loves hunting. They aren't needy, these people. They're independent and I'm not like that and I didn't tell him "I love you" quick enough.

Now it's too late.

I race back to my cave with the leather pieces in my hands, and I fling them down and throw the privacy screen up the moment I cross the threshold. I fight back a sob, pressing my palms to my eyes.

There's a scratch at the screen. "Megan? Come out so we can talk." It's Georgie, and she's using her Reasonable-Tribe-Leader voice, acting as if nothing's wrong. "Don't be like this."

I don't want to talk to her. I just want to hide.

Even if she tells me they don't think I did it, I know some of them did. There will always be that doubt. After all, Ariana cried a few too many times and now some of the hunters think she's a whiner. Josie gets called "noisy" because she talks a lot and puts on an enthusiastic air when she's nervous. Am I going to be the food thief forever? The pig that can't control herself around the food stores?

No matter what happens, I'm going to get pegged as a problem because I made a stupid joke to Farli. Because no one trusts me. Because I don't really fit in.

I ignore another scratch at the privacy screen, and for once, I'm really glad that those screens are sacrosanct in the tribe. Georgie can't barge her way in and talk to me; everyone would frown on that as the height of rudeness. I can be by myself, and I can think.

And right now...I think I need to leave.

I sniff, then look in our small pile of stored goods for a bag. There are lots of caves in this place. I can learn to live in one by myself if I have to. I know how to make fire, and how to look at tracks, and I can fish and...and...

And just be alone for the rest of my life.

I crumple on the furs, weeping.

21

CASHOL

When I return to the cave, something is amiss. Meh-gan is not near the fire like she usually is, watching for me. I have grown used to seeing her eyes light up at my return, and I am hungry for the smile that curves her pretty mouth. Instead, there is a group standing near the fire, talking quietly, and all look miserable. Nearby, Jo-see scrapes a skin in silence.

Now I know something is wrong for Jo-see to be silent.

My traps were empty this day, and so I return with nothing. I head over to my cave, and notice that the privacy screen is up. Is my mate napping? Is she unwell? Frowning, I look over at the group near the fire, and immediately, Shorshie heads for me. She has a worried expression on her face and pulls me aside. "There's a small problem," she whispers. "Can we talk?"

I shrug and let her pull me with her, casting a longing look in my cave's direction. If Meh-gan is asleep, I should like to wake her with my mouth between her soft thighs. "Let us speak quickly."

"I think Megan thinks we hate her."

That snaps my attention back to Vektal's mate. "What?"

She twists her hands and makes a face, then quickly tells me of what happened earlier. "No one was accusing her of anything. You know Farli's young and probably thought Megan was serious with that joke, but no one really blames Megan. I tried to talk to her and she threw the screen up, but I can hear her crying." Shorshie looks upset. "Everyone is just devastated they made her cry. Please, please let her know that no one blames her?"

I nod, racing toward my cave. I was glad to see the privacy screen when I arrived, but now it seems ominous. I push it aside, looking for my mate, and immediately see she is at the back of the cave, stuffing things into a pack. Her face is wet with tears and her eyes are red-rimmed and miserable.

"Meh-gan, my mate. What is wrong?"

She looks up at me, her eyes full of pure misery, and a fresh round of tears bursts from her. "Nothing."

Are we back to this, then? "If you say nothing is wrong, my pretty one, then why are you packing a bag?" I sit down next to her and pull it out of her arms.

She takes it back. "I think I have to leave."

"Leave?"

Her hands shake as she swipes at her eyes. "I can't stay here if I'm a problem."

"No one thinks you are a problem—"

"You don't know that!" she cries, heartbroken. "You weren't here!"

"I know what Shorshie has told me," I say calmly, steadily. I need to be reasonable for her, to be strong, even though all I want to do is jump out of the cave and yell at Shorshie and the others for making my Meh-gan cry. I pull the bag out of her arms one more time and take her hands in mine, holding them tightly. "But I would like to hear what you have to tell me, my mate. Will you speak of what happened that has made you so sad?"

Tearfully, she recounts what happened this afternoon, and her worries. She tells me about how she should have never joked about the food, that she would never touch it. She feels that if she stays, she will always be blamed whenever there is a problem. She feels this cannot be a home for her now.

It seems such a small thing to be so upset over, but my Meh-gan is devastated. She has already worried that her position in the tribe is tenuous, and this only hurts her heart even more. No matter how much Shorshie insists that Meh-gan is not to blame, my Meh-gan will blame herself. And she is right to a certain extent...we are a small tribe. How often do we tease Harrec about how he faints at the sight of his blood? How much is shy Zennek teased for his confident, sultry mate, or Dagesh for the noises he and No-rah enthusiastically make in the privacy of their own cave? Someone is bound to joke.

Only Meh-gan will not find it funny. It will hurt her spirit.

And so I must fix this, because I cannot bear the sight of my mate's sadness. It tears me up inside.

I cup her sweet face. "Do not cry, my resonance. It will be all right."

"I just..." she hiccups. "I would never..."

"I know." I stroke her cheeks with my thumbs. "I know you would not. Shorshie knows you would not. Everyone knows you would not. They see you working every day. You do not sit around and wait for others to feed you. No one thinks you would destroy food just to be cruel."

"But Farli—"

"Is a kit. When I was a kit, I believed that my mother was in the Ancestors' Cave because my father had said she joined the ancestors after giving birth to me. So I thought that if I ran away and went there on my own, I would find her." I give her a smile. "My father could not believe my foolishness. Kits are full of foolish thoughts, my mate. No one truly believes Farli's words, I promise."

"Farli is sa-khui," Meh-gan says softly. "I'm not. That makes it different."

"You are not leaving the tribe over a few roots," I promise her. "They are easily replaced. I will dig them up tomorrow and fill the storage cave once more. Problem solved."

The tears threatening to spill over her eyes again abate, just a little. "You...you will?" She sniffles.

She looks so surprised that my pride is wounded. Why is she shocked I would do this? She feels responsible, so it is my duty as her mate to ensure she is happy. "Have I not always said that we are together? We are one? I will not allow anyone to speak poorly of my mate. No one will ever doubt you." I give her a fierce look. "Not to my face."

Meh-gan sobs and flings her arms around my neck. "Why are you so good to me?"

I pat her back awkwardly. Why am I good to her? "Because I am your mate. It is my job to make you smile...and it seems I am doing a terrible job of it this day."

She gives a watery laugh. "Are you kidding? You always make me smile."

Not enough, I think, and I vow to do more.

MEH-GAN SLEEPS FITFULLY THAT EVENING, CURLED UP AGAINST ME and holding onto my arm as if she is terrified I will abandon her halfway through the night. I listen to her shuddery breathing, holding her tight against me, and wish that I could take away her worry.

To think that my mate has been so upset over roots, of all

things. It baffles the mind and yet…I understand it. Meh-gan so desperately wants to feel safe and secure with her place in the tribe, and every setback feels enormous.

I pepper her face with kisses as she wakes up, and wring a small smile from her. "I am going root hunting today," I promise. "Do you wish to come?"

She shakes her head, and I am not entirely surprised. "I think I'll just hide in here, if that's all right. Maybe…maybe take a nap." Meh-gan gives me a faint smile.

"Nap…or work on presents to give to everyone to ensure that they like you?" I know my mate far too well and already she is eyeing her basket of leather projects.

Her mouth twitches and she nudges my shoulder. "Maybe. I don't know."

"If they do not love you like I do, then they are the fools," I promise, and kiss her palm.

Meh-gan sucks in a breath, her eyes wide. "You…you love me?"

"You doubt this?" I put her hand over my heart dramatically. "I have loved you since the moment I first saw you. You looked at me as if you could not tell if you wished to scowl at me or smile at me…and you smiled." I grin. "But it was a smile that promised you would gut me if I crossed you. That was when I knew my heart was no longer mine."

Her mouth trembles. "You're too good for me."

"No, I am exactly the mate you deserve." I nibble on her palm again. "Some would say that is a curse."

She giggles. Just a little, but it is enough.

22

CASHOL

*I*t is hard to leave her side, but eventually I must go out. There are roots to be gathered and stored, before anyone can even think to comment on what happened yesterday. The others in the tribe give me uncertain looks when I emerge, and I see Kemli near the fire, sewing a tunic, a sad expression on her face. She gives me a hopeful glance, then looks over at our cave, where the privacy screen is up again, and her expression changes to one of sadness again.

Kemli is so motherly, she probably thinks she is to blame. Meh-gan's tears probably upset Kemli as much as they do me.

"My cousin," Vektal calls, jogging up to me. "Where do you go this morning?"

I gesture at the packs I have slung over my shoulder. "On a most dangerous hunt," I joke. "I am gathering roots to fill the supply cave again."

Vektal purses his lips, then nods. "May we speak before you go?"

"Of course."

My cousin accompanies me out of the cave and into the snow. The day is a pleasant one, the twin suns casting their light down on the glittering landscape. It is such a shame that so many days are full of flying snow, because that means my Meh-gan must stay inside where it is warm. On a day like today, it is a good day to go fishing...and yet she will not leave our cave. I fight back a sigh of frustration. Perhaps I will finish my task early and then we can spend what is left of the day together.

"So..." Vektal says when we are alone. "Georgie tells me Meh-gan thinks everyone blames her."

I nod. "She feels uncertain of her place with us and this does not help. I go to get roots so she will worry less about what was destroyed."

Vektal crosses his arms over his chest and gazes out at the distant cliffs. "No one blames her. Does she truly think that we believe she chewed through the storage baskets to taste each root?"

I shrug. "It does not matter what we believe, only what Meh-gan believes." I pause. "And what the rest of the tribe believes."

"No one thinks she did it." Vektal shakes his head. "Kemli is devastated. Even now she feels she is to blame and is making a tunic for Meh-gan to try to apologize."

I suspected as much. "That is thoughtful of her. Meh-gan will be surprised."

"Georgie cried," Vektal says flatly. "I did not like it."

"She cried?"

He nods, his jaw set into a grim line. "She feels it is her fault, too. I have not said anything to the others because Kemli will make another tunic out of guilt and she already has enough to do."

"Meh-gan will be upset that Shorshie is sad," I admit. "I am not sure I should tell her."

"Do not. They are both carrying kits. Everything makes them cry." He exhales deeply, as if tired. "The night before, Georgie cried because her feet were cold. And before that, she cried because she missed something called kah-fee." He shakes his head. "I tell you this because you and Meh-gan recently resonated. Now that she is carrying your kit, her mood will be very...tender. You should expect many tears." He rubs a hand down his face. "Many, many tears."

I laugh at my cousin's frustrated expression. "Is this why you are so eager to hunt some mornings?"

Vektal gives me a wary look. "They cannot help it. It is the kit that makes them weepy."

Perhaps that is part of the reason that Meh-gan is so upset, but I know it goes deeper. She desperately wants to feel secure with her spot in the tribe, and now she does not. It does not matter that it is not a big deal in my eyes, because it is a big deal in hers....and so I will fix it. I hold one of the empty packs out to my cousin. "You can go root hunting with me if you like."

He takes the bag immediately. "I think this is a good idea." He pauses, and then admits in a low voice, "Georgie cried this morning because she did not like the way I looked at her in a dream she had." He shakes his head. "Be ready, cousin. Be ready for tears."

I just laugh again. Hearing this makes me feel a little better, but I will not rest until Meh-gan is satisfied....even if it takes until our kit is born.

MEGAN

I'm a little afraid to leave the cave in the afternoon. I hide in there all morning, busying myself with work, but a few people come by to visit and scratch at the screen, but I turn them all away, calling out that I have a headache. It's such a bad lie but I don't care. My head does hurt, just from the stress. And I'm not ready to talk to anyone just yet. Not even Josie, whose chirpy voice tells me that she has no idea what's going on or what I'm upset over. In a way, that's good. It means people aren't gossiping.

But it also makes me feel like I can't talk to anyone.

Well, other than Cashol, but he's out right now cleaning up "my" mess.

My heart fills with affection for him. He's been so good to me. He hasn't made me feel like I'm to blame, or that I'm crazy for getting upset. He just hugged me and promised to fix it. I don't deserve someone as good and caring as him...but I'm lucky that my cootie chose him for me anyhow.

When I first got here, I used to imagine what it'd be like to be mated to each guy. What life would be like with someone as silent and calm as Warrek, or as volatile as Bek, as hot-tempered as Hassen, who acts first and thinks later. I can't picture any of them now, not now that I know what Cashol is like, how he can be funny and goofy and sometimes sly, or achingly thoughtful and sweet. How utterly supportive he is. How he always tries to make me happy, as if he's got no other goal in life than to be my biggest supporter.

I'm so fucking lucky to have him. I swipe at my eyes, because they feel leaky all over again. Would anyone else make me feel this way? So supported? So loved?

Never.

In that moment, I realize it's all going to be okay. Not because of something I do, but because Cashol will make it okay. If someone gives me shit or says I was the problem with the food, he'll be all charming and teasing and make them feel silly, or he'll just fix it. He won't let anyone toss me out on my ass because he's got a way of getting what he wants. And I know he wants me happy.

My heart feels full at the realization, and I spend all afternoon thinking about what a wonderful person my mate is. I can't wait for him to come home so I can see his big smile crease his narrow face, to hear him joke about something, to tease me about my fascination with feet. It's just his feet that do something to me, though.

Just like his smile makes everything in the day better. His laugh makes me feel joy. His touch makes me breathless.

I miss him fiercely, and I hate that he's been gone all day. I want to kiss him. I want to curl up in his lap and have him hold me. I want to slide my hand into the front of his pants and give him the same release he gives me every day, just because he likes going down on me. I shiver and clench my thighs together at the thought, feeling achy and needy. When he comes home tonight, I'm gonna give him the best damn welcome, I decide. A nice, delicious dinner, a mate that's thrilled to see him, and then I'm going to seduce the hell out of him.

Not because I think it's what he wants, or what's expected of me, but because I want to do it. Because I'm excited to touch him. Because I'm hungry for more of his warmth, his laughter, his body, the way he groans when he touches me, as if he never knew something could be so damn good.

Just thinking about him makes me breathless.

I put a few fuel chips on the fire, stoking the flames, and start making tea. The suns should be going down, and hopefully Cashol will be home soon. I smooth my hand over my hair, and as I do, I hear a distant conversation.

It sounds a bit like my mate.

I move to the screen in front of my cave's entrance and peek out. Sure enough, there's my mate, two packs utterly bulging full of roots on his back. Vektal is nearby, but sees Georgie and immediately veers toward her in a way that makes my heart melt for my friend. Cashol heads for the supply cave, no doubt to drop off his load, and I emerge from our cave, happy to see him.

He's getting the best damn foot rub tonight, I decide.

Before I can get to the supply cave, I hear voices. I pause, then move to the cave wall, hiding in the shadows so I can eavesdrop. I know I shouldn't, but I can't help myself.

"That is a great many roots," I hear Asha say, and inwardly I cringe. Asha is about my age, but she's gorgeous and one of the few sa-khui females so she tends to swan around like a queen bee. I avoid her, because I know she has a sharp tongue and a bitter outlook. The fact that she's there to talk to Cashol is not good.

"We need a great many," another voice says, and I recognize Bek. Ugh. This just went from bad to worse. He sounds a little bitter. "Since a great many were ruined."

My stomach clenches and I feel tears threaten.

"It was not my mate, so do not even suggest it," Cashol's voice is clear and loud, and brooks absolutely no argument. "Do not even think it."

I'm such a dork, because I absolutely squirm with pleasure to hear him say that.

"Who else would say such a foolish thing?" Bek asks.

"Be fair," Asha says, and I'm surprised to hear that. "We have all done silly things in the past. I left the lids off the baskets once, and old Drenol gave me a tongue lashing I did not forget. Sometimes we do not mean to cause problems, but they just happen. No one is to blame. There is no malice involved."

I'm surprised that Asha is defending me. I don't think we've ever said two words to each other, but I'm filled with warmth that she has my back, even without me knowing it.

"Bah." Bek says. "Now we must all work harder because she was careless."

"She was not careless." Cashol's voice is crisp and strong and without a hint of its normal teasing. If anything, he sounds irritated. "And do not suggest such a thing to me, Bek. You know no one works harder than my mate. Admit it is so."

There is a long pause.

Then, "She is a hard worker," Bek admits grudgingly. "I did not mean to imply otherwise."

"My Meh-gan is worth more than everything in this storage cave," Cashol says, utterly firm and confident in what he's saying. "If it would make her happy, I would toss all of this out into the snow and gather it again, just to make her smile. I only hunt these roots because she worries we will think badly of her and the tribe is important to her. I do not replace them out of guilt. I replace them to ease her mind."

I press my fingertips to my lips, surprised. He sounds so very angry. So pissed that they even dare to mention my name.

"It is just silliness in a tribe that likes to chatter too much around a fire," Asha says casually. "Everyone likes your pretty mate. Ease that kink out of your tail, Cashol. We mean no harm."

"You think you mean no harm, but even careless words can hurt. The humans do not think like we do, and I will not have her upset by anyone in this tribe, understand?" Cashol's practically growling at them. He's scolding them. For me.

I am filled with so much damn love for that man right now.

The moment the thought ripples through my brain, I know it's true. I love Cashol. I adore him. He makes me so damn happy. Even when I'm stressed or worried, he makes me feel like it'll be all right as long as he's right there with me. I love him, and I love his caring spirit, how he jokes and teases but he's always one hundred percent on my side...no matter who he's talking to. Just like I can't imagine resonating to anyone else, I can't imagine sharing the rest of my life with anyone else —on Earth or here.

Earth guys aren't made like Cashol. They might be smoking hot and built, they might be rippling with abs, or teasing and charming. They might be utterly devoted to a girl...but they're never all those things at once. Cashol's everything I ever wanted or needed.

My eyes brim with tears again, but this time it's not because I'm sad, it's because I feel like shouting with pure joy. I want to shout at the rest of the tribe—*that's my man!*

But they'll just think I'm crazy. *Of course he is your man,* I can imagine one of the elders saying, a look of genuine puzzlement on their weathered faces. *No one would think otherwise.*

"We understand," Asha says from inside the cave, interrupting my giddy thoughts. "Come, Bek, let us leave Cashol alone before he starts attacking us for breathing wrong." She chuckles, and Bek grunts, and there's a shuffling sound inside.

I sink into the shadows, not wanting them to notice that I'm here. That I listened in on everything. The sa-khui don't care much about eavesdropping, but they like to pretend privacy to give people their space, even when we're all living in a cave together, and I don't want to make Asha and Bek uncomfortable. I wait for them to leave, Asha talking about the upcoming brutal season and the heavy snows it will bring. They head toward the large central area of the cave, and as they do, I slip into the supply cavern. At the back of the cave, kneeling beside a few baskets, Cashol works to fill them with the large, round not-potatoes. I glance around me. There's an old privacy screen by the entrance, the decorative stitches on it faded and a rip in the corner. Someone must have made a new one and discarded this one, but it works for my purposes. I grab it and put it over the entrance.

Suddenly, it's really dark in the cave, almost all of the light gone.

"What?" Cashol asks, clear surprise in his voice. He calls out. "Someone is in here."

He must not see me then, the shadows being too deep. I

move forward in the darkness, my fingers brushing his hair. "It's me," I whisper.

"Meh-gan?" I can feel him turn in surprise. "Did you just awaken? I am putting these away but I will not be long—"

I slide my hand along his jaw in the darkness and then press my fingertips to his lips. "Shhh. You have to keep your voice down."

"And why is that?" There's amusement in his tone.

"Because I'm going to seduce you in here," I whisper, and lean in, licking the shell of his ear. "And I don't want them to hear us, so you're going to need to be quiet."

23

MEGAN

There's the sound of breath catching, and then Cashol lets out a low groan, his hand sliding to my waist, and then lower, to my backside. "What...what brought this on? Not that I am displeased—"

I chuckle, moving my hands to the front of his vest. He wears very little when he goes out, which means he's going to be easy to strip naked. "I heard you defending me to Asha and Bek, and it made me realize just how damn wonderful you are and how much I love you. Thank you for believing in me." I'm just blown away by how wonderful he is. Not only did he spend all day getting roots, but when he got back, he wasn't even cranky. He was just frustrated at them for even thinking I might be guilty.

There are no words to describe how much I love this man.

"Of course I would defend you," he whispers, and I can hear just how puzzled he is that I would even think otherwise.

"I just don't want you to feel as if you have to choose me over them—"

His soft chuckle cuts me off and he tugs me into his lap. The darkness makes it impossible to see his face, but I can just imagine his bright smile. "It will never happen, because you are part of the tribe, my silly female. And if you left, I would follow you. It is that simple."

I can scarcely breathe. "You would?"

"Of course I would. You have my heart." He takes my hand and presses it to his chest.

"I love you," I whisper to him. "I love you so fucking much." I slide my hand down his front and cup his cock, just like I've been aching to do for weeks. "Now will you let me have sex with you?"

He groans, tangling his hand in my hair as he pulls me toward him for a kiss. "Yes. Lie down on your back and—"

"No," I whisper, and stroke his cock again. He's already hard and swelling against my hand, so perfectly thick and gorgeous that my mouth waters. I lean in and nip his lip, kissing him teasingly. "I'm making love to *you*."

I kiss him, and his tongue flicks against mine, as if he's licking me. I let out a shuddery little moan of pleasure as his mouth captures mine, and then the kiss becomes a tug of war. I lose myself in the feel of his mouth, in the sweep of his tongue, until the world ceases to exist outside of the pleasure of Cashol's mouth. I bury my hands in his hair, brushing up against his horns, and he grabs me and holds me against him, as if he can't bear to have me be even an inch away. I rock my hips against his lap, and he's so hard and straining through his leathers.

I moan into his mouth and drag myself over his length. "Why do you always feel so good?"

"Because I am yours," he tells me. "You know you belong to me and I belong to you."

I can't argue with that kind of reasoning. I move against him, rocking against the length of him as we kiss, until he's panting, and when I move, he thrusts up against me.

Enough teasing, I decide. I want all of him.

I lift my hips just enough to give us some space, and then pull at the laces that hold his leggings together. His clothes fall loose, and I shove them down, uncovering his straining cock and that fascinating spur I've wanted to experience again. "Looks like you missed me," I tease, trying to be flirty.

"Every moment I was away from you was painful," he admits. "I wanted you in my arms. If not that, then by my side." He pulls at my tunic and we pause to tug it over my head. The moment I'm free of it, his big, warm hands are on my breasts and I have to bite back a moan of pleasure. They're so sensitive lately, and his hands feel incredible.

Hungry, I kiss him with all the frantic passion racing through me, and it's like he knows just what to do to make me wild. His fingers move over the tips of my breasts, teasing them with feather-light touches that make me ache deep inside my core. I take him in my hand, stroking his thick length and whimpering against his mouth as he teases my breasts to aching, tight points.

"This is mine," I tell him as I stroke his cock, dragging my fingers through the pre-cum slicking the head of it. "Mine and only mine."

"Yours," he pants, pinching my nipples as if he's determined to make me crazy before I can make him come. "It rises for no one but you."

"Good." I say it a little viciously, but I get an intense thrill at the realization that this big, gorgeous man is mine and no one else can do to him what I do.

I lean in and taste his lips again, fascinated by their softness in a man that seems to be all angles and muscle. I taste him with small nips, drawing at his lower lip over and over again, until he's groaning underneath me, his hands cupping and teasing my breasts until I feel as if I might break from the sheer pleasure of it.

"Feed your teats to me." Cashol drags me up to his mouth, lifting me in his arms, and I want to laugh at his phrasing... except I'm far too turned on. With a tiny sigh, I sit up and rub my breasts against his face, whimpering when he latches onto one and works my nipple with his clever tongue. "You are so beautiful," he murmurs between licks.

"It's dark in here. You can't see how I look."

"You taste beautiful," he amends. His hand moves to my other breast, and then he's teasing both of them as I writhe on his lap. He feels huge in the darkness, all warm muscle and hard cock, and I can't stop the noises I make as he teases me. I breathe in sharply as he takes one nipple into his mouth and sucks hard, my body lighting up at that pleasure-pain moment. He releases it with a little pop, and then licks the sensitive spot. "So beautiful."

"I want you," I tell him, and shift my weight so I'm no longer sitting so high in his lap. I reach between us and stroke his cock again. "Want you inside me, Cashol."

"Take your leathers off," he demands, and he sounds so bossy and confident that it makes me utterly wet. My laughing, teasing Cashol has been replaced by this authoritative, demanding man, and I love it.

With a little moan, I get to my feet and start to strip off my pants. The moment I have them around my thighs, his arms lock around my hips and he drags me forward.

"Want you on my tongue." Cashol pulls me toward him and I stagger, supporting my hands on his horns. "Give me your cunt, my mate."

I suck in a breath at those words. I can't resist, though. I want him—and that—too much. So I hold onto him, lifting one foot onto one of the baskets behind him. I feel his hot breath on my skin a split second before his mouth is there, and then I lose all rational thought as he licks my pussy. I can't even be embarrassed; it feels too good to have his mouth dipping between my legs, nuzzling at my sensitive folds.

And when he finds my clit? I nearly come undone.

He locks an arm around me, holding me in place as he uses the tip of his ridged tongue to draw small circles in just the perfect spot, teasing and toying with the sensitive skin until I'm shuddering with need and every muscle in my body is locking up.

"Yes," he breathes, lifting his head. "Come on my face, my mate. I want to taste all of you."

I pull away.

I can come on his face. Heck, I do at least once a day right now, because he's so eager to go down on me (and I'm pretty damn eager to let him). But if I do, I don't want us to be finished. I want him deep inside me. I don't want this to just be my pleasure. I want this to be a pleasure we share together.

So I slide out of his grip, ignoring his protests, and sink back down to his lap. I straddle him, rocking my drenched folds against his hot length, and I kiss him. "I want you inside me when I come," I whisper.

He groans my name.

"I'm here," I tell him, even though it feels unnecessary. His grip on my hips feels needy, frantic, as if he's afraid I'm going to leave...or as if I'm a dream that he has to cling to so he doesn't wake up. It reminds me how long Cashol's been alone—utterly alone. Other than his cousin, he's had no family to love him for years and years. "I'm here," I promise him again. "I have you."

The breath explodes from him when I lower myself onto his cock. "Meh-gan," he chokes out, his hands digging into my skin. "My Meh-gan."

"Yours. All yours." I work my way down his length, inch by glorious inch. He feels too big, but in all the best sorts of ways, and I bite my lip as he stretches my body. I move my hips with small motions, trying to work him deeper and deeper, until the world around me seems to shrink to just the feel of him penetrating me while I sink down upon him.

Cashol lets out a shuddering breath as I take him to the hilt, and he kisses me.

I moan into his mouth, remaining completely still, losing myself to the sensations. Of his cock, so big and thick I feel impaled and full and utterly aware of every single nerve ending in my body. Of the spur that's somehow perfectly slid into place against my clit. Of his warm, suede-skin under mine. His mouth, hot and needy on my own. His khui, humming the softest of songs as if it's pleased by what we're doing.

In the darkness, everything is tactile, and that makes it ten times more intense.

"Ride me," he murmurs against my lips. "Claim me as yours."

With another whimper, I do exactly as he says. I lift my hips, rising up and then pushing back down onto him. Our bodies make a wet noise, and I'm too caught up in him to care. My lips part and I gasp as he thrusts up when I move down, and then he's hammering into me, taking control despite the fact that I'm on top of him.

We crash into each other, me pushing down as he pumps upward, and I'm crying out at the sensations rippling through me. I can't bear it—it's too much to feel the ridges on his cock, the thickness of it, and the spur that prods and slicks against my clit over and over again. I stiffen, breathing his name as I come, and he bites down on my shoulder with a low groan as he comes a few moments later. There's a gentle spreading warmth between our joined bodies, and I give him an exhausted, open-mouthed kiss of wonder.

"I love you," I tell him.

"You have my heart...and my cock."

I chuckle at that. "Thanks, I think. It's the pairing I've always wanted."

He laughs, and I feel it all the way through me. It sends a shiver up my spine, my inner walls rippling against the still-too-big-feeling intrusion of his cock. "I am amazed by you, my Meh-gan," he murmurs, cupping my face and kissing my brow.

"Me? Why?"

"Because you have trapped me in the supply cave and straddled me until my brains have leaked out of my cock." He kisses along my jaw. "And yet I still crave more of your touch."

I slide my arms around his neck, curling a finger into his thick hair. I know how he feels. Sex has always been fun and pleasant, but it's never made me feel like I was coming apart and suddenly whole again—like I do right now with him. I want to hold him down and do all kinds of degenerate things to this gorgeous man, just to blow his mind and make him realize everything that's possible. "I feel the same...but I'm pretty sure someone is going to want something in here soon, so maybe we should go back to our cave."

Cashol chuckles and kisses along my jaw. "As if they have not already heard us? It is not as if we are quiet when we come together."

No, I imagine we aren't. Maybe not as loud as Nora and Dagesh, but definitely not quiet.

"And do you think we are the first ones to be swept up with the need to mate the moment we are alone together?" He nips lightly at my ear, making me moan—and the deep parts of me shudder with need. "I have caught others in this very same storage cave. Sometimes you cannot wait to put your hands on your mate."

"I guess not." It's definitely a tribe that doesn't feel shy in showing their affection for one another. "We should probably head back anyhow," I say, stroking my fingers over his nipple. "Before they think I really am eating all the roots here."

He snorts. "Asha would beat anyone over the head for suggesting such a thing. And I would, too."

I make a mental note to work harder at befriending Asha.

※

WE RELUCTANTLY PULL APART AND DRESS IN THE DARKNESS, stealing kisses from each other as we do. Cashol pulls me against him and then tugs up my tunic, his mouth on my nipple before I can catch my breath, and it takes everything I have not to fling him back to the floor and have my way with him. I'm aching and aroused all over again by the time he lets me go and pulls my tunic back down. I'm a little overly slick between my thighs, but in a way, I also like it. It reminds me that I was just thoroughly claimed by my mate...

Who also looks thoroughly pleased with himself, I can't help but notice as Cashol eases the screen out of the cave entrance and the light of the main cave floods in. It outlines his messy hair, his kiss-swollen lips that I've thoroughly tasted in the last hour or so, and the fact that his cock is straining at the front of his leggings again. He adjusts the decorative flap to hide that, grins at me, and then looks at someone just outside the cave. "Have you been there long, little Farli?"

"Long enough," the girl chirps, and I fight back a sound of dismay. Oh god. I'm polluting young minds by debauching my fine-ass mate in public. Now we have to do the walk of shame back to our cave, and I'm absolutely sure I look like I just got fucked hard. My hair's a mess, my nipples are so stiff that they're sending shivers through my body as they rub against the leather of my tunic, and I don't even want to think how my leggings are holding up.

But then Cashol offers me his hand, that big grin on his face, and I don't care what I look like. I put my hand in his and smile, letting him lead me forward.

Farli giggles at the sight of us, a knowing look on her young face. "I was going to ask if you were hunting the hopper, but then she groaned your name and I figured you were doing other things."

I bury my face against Cashol's arm, my cheeks burning.

He laughs, and then pauses. "Hopper? What hopper?"

Farli chortles with glee. "Why, the hopper! The one that took a bite out of all of the roots we had stored. He ate through three baskets, too. Vaza saw his hind end earlier today and we've been trying to catch him all afternoon." She puts her hands out, gesturing. "You should see him. He is huge! At least this big."

"Of course he is," Cashol laughs. "He has eaten all the roots." He slides his arm around me and glances down at my face.

I'm sure it shows how utterly thunderstruck I am. "A hopper," I repeat slowly. "In the supply cave."

"Yes!" Farli is all enthusiasm. "He must have snuck inside somehow. Vaza says he is going to go into the stewpot next! I want to catch it before he does, though." She beams a bright smile at us and then wriggles her way past into the storage cave, where not five minutes ago, I was defiling my handsome mate.

Of course it was a hopper. That makes so much sense. It chewed through baskets and ate a bite out of roots here and there. A simple answer, and now everyone knows it wasn't me. I'm just...flabbergasted.

"A hopper," I say to Cashol.

He steers me toward our cave, heading to our home. "I told you no one thought it was you. It was only your fear that made you panic."

He's right, though I feel a little silly. Okay, a lot silly. "I'm sorry I made such a big deal—"

"Do not be sorry." He just shakes his head, moving toward our cave before anyone else can stop us and talk to us. There's a lot of people out right now, and I'm sure some of them are looking in our direction, but Cashol's paying attention to only me. He gently steers me inside our cave and then puts the privacy screen up. "It felt like a big problem to you, and so it was a big problem."

"I...might be a little weepy thanks to the baby." I wring my hands, feeling utterly foolish. Of course no one thought I took a bite out of each root and put it back. That's just freaking stupid. I feel so dumb right now. I completely overreacted.

"You might be," Cashol agrees. "Vektal tells me that Shorshie was mad at him over something he did in her dream. So you are not the only one that has unreasonable moments."

I giggle at that. "Okay, I feel a little better knowing I'm not the only hormonal beast."

"You are not a hormonal beast," he says, pulling me into his arms.

"If you say I'm 'your' beast I'm going to kick you," I warn him, recognizing the teasing look in his eyes.

"You are not." Cashol smiles and brushes a lock of hair back from my face. "You are my treasure, worth more than all the mah-nee in your world."

I suck in a breath, because that might be the sweetest thing anyone has ever said to me...and it turns me on like crazy. "Do you...want a foot rub?" I offer. "For being such a good mate?"

He gives me a sly look. "Is my foot the only thing getting rubbed?"

"What do you think?"

Cashol pretends to consider. "I think I will rub your foot, you will rub mine, and then you will climb on top of me like you did earlier." His eyes flare hot with arousal. "And then we will both curl up in the furs and anticipate a fat hopper stew."

I laugh, my heart feeling foolish and yet utterly light with joy. "It's a deal."

24

NOW

MEGAN

When I finish telling Josie the cleaned up version of how we met, she makes an exclamation of sheer disgust. "I can't believe you hid all this from me!"

"You didn't ask!" I protest back, and she scowls so darkly at me that for a moment I think we're going to have a pregnant lady brawl right here in her tiny hut. "Seriously, it didn't occur to me to be all 'Hey, Jos, back when Cashol and I first got together, I was hella clingy and a real nutcase because I felt like I didn't belong.'" I shrug. "What did you want me to say?"

"You could have told me, Meggers! I thought we were best friends!" Her petite face screws up and she looks like she can't decide if she wants to punch me or cry. "I had no idea and now I feel like the worst friend ever. You guys were always so kissy-kissy every time I saw you that I thought everything was perfect."

"Well, sure. I wanted everyone to think we were perfect," I remind her. "That was part of the stress of it all. Besides, you were so busy hating Haeden's guts that you probably wouldn't have noticed anyhow. Remember how long it took for us to realize Aehako and Kira were a thing?"

She chuckles. "All right, I guess that's fair. I—" Her breath hisses between her teeth and I swear her belly ripples. Her hand goes to the front of her massive stomach and she shifts on her pillow, wincing.

"Are you in labor?" I ask, getting to my feet. "Is the baby coming? Should I go have someone fetch Haeden?"

Her grimace turns to a rueful smile and she rubs the small of her back again. "It's been coming for days and days now but no baby yet. Just loads of contractions, spaced too far apart for anything to happen." Josie tilts her ungainly body, then raises her arms. "Help me get up?"

I help haul her to her feet and she begins to waddle back and forth, pacing, her hands at the small of her back as if it can somehow support the enormous belly she's sporting. She gives me a game smile and rubs her stomach, and even though she's uncomfortable right now, I know Josie loves this. She wants a huge family and she's so in love with Haeden that she still gets starry-eyed whenever he walks into her sights. It's really cute. "Kemli told me that one of her babies was like this," Josie offers as she paces around the room slowly. "That she had a week of nothing but cramps and then boom, the baby shot out in like five minutes."

"Well, that sounds awful." I don't mind being pregnant, but I'm not remembering labor too fondly. I rub my own, much smaller belly, and the baby underneath flutters as if to reassure me. "A week of labor? No thanks."

Josie huffs another laugh. "Oh please. You'd change places with me right now if it meant holding your baby that much faster."

We exchange a look, and I have to admit she's right. "Point taken. So...since this one is almost here, what does it feel like to you now? Boy or girl?" Josie and I have talked about babies constantly in the last few months...okay, last few turns of the seasons. It's hard not to be baby obsessed when you have a little one, or when you resonate again. Josie gets it, and I'm glad we're friends and live next to each other so we can talk babies all we want.

I do know that one thing she hasn't done is ask the healer what the baby is. Sometimes Maylak can tell, and sometimes she can't. Josie hasn't asked, and I haven't either. It's nice to have an exciting surprise to look forward to, and I know Josie feels the same. Mine has felt like a girl all this time. I carry her slightly different in my belly, I crave different foods than when I was pregnant with Holvek, and I just...feel like it's a girl. Josie's carried both a boy and a girl, so I'm always surprised that she can't tell with this one. Some weeks she's positive it's a girl, and then sometimes she's utterly certain that it's a boy.

Josie rubs her belly as she waddles around the hearth, considering. "This week I feel like it's a boy. I was craving hraku seeds earlier today, and I really wanted those when I was pregnant with Joden, remember?"

"Um, hraku seeds are delicious. When are we not craving them?" I give her a strange look. "You know that doesn't mean anything."

She shrugs. "I know. You're still positive yours is a girl, huh?"

"Pretty sure." It feels weird to sit by the fire while Josie paces around me. "You want me to get you anything? Some tea? A snack? The healer?"

"Naaah." Josie just waddles a bit more, lost in thought. "What was the first baby you were pregnant with? The one you lost? A boy or a girl?"

My throat gets tight for a moment, and I shrug. "It was too

early to tell. I was supposed to go back to the doctor in a few days to have a blood test, but I never made it." I shrug. "I like to think it was a girl, though."

"Did you have a name picked out for that girl? Maybe you can re-use it. I know you guys haven't been able to decide on a name. Maybe honor her with that one."

I know Josie means well, but the thought makes me hurt. I lost my baby. It was taken from me. Giving her name to another baby feels...cruel. I want her to keep her name as hers and hers alone, because that way, I'll never forget her.

It would feel wrong to re-use the name Aurora. So I'll come up with a new one. "I'll let Cashol keep trying to come up with a name. Maybe he'll hit on a good one."

Josie makes a face. "And maybe dirtbeaks fly out of my ass. You know he's terrible at it."

We both laugh, because he really, really is. I know he's terrible on purpose, but still.

She puts a hand to her forehead, and she looks really tired for a moment. "I've had a hell of a time thinking of a name for this one myself. We're struggling to find the right name combination."

"Jasen?" I suggest. I love the name, but it doesn't work for me and Cashol. "For a boy?"

Josie beams. "I love that, but it sounds awfully close to Joden and Joha. They're too similar as it is. I've taken to calling the baby Jojo sometimes and they both answer. It makes Haeden crazy." She smiles fondly. "I can't imagine another J-name in the mix."

"It only matters what you like," I point out. "Everyone else in the tribe can just deal with it. If you like Jasen, go with Jasen. All the sa-khui sound far too similar anyhow. Another J name would totally be on brand."

"Another J name might drive my poor mate up the wall. We need something different, I just don't know what." She winces, rubs the underside of her belly, and keeps walking. "You should probably be heading home soon, shouldn't you? I've kept you all morning."

"I'm good," I promise her. "Cashol went hunting with Holvek. If you don't mind the company, I'm happy to stay."

She gives me a wide smile of gratitude. "I'd love the company. It helps me think about things other than this." Josie gestures at her bulk.

So we settle in and drink more tea, and as we do, I get out bits of leather and write down letters on each leather fragment, using a bit of coal to mark them. I spell out her name and an approximation of Haeden's name—since the sa-khui have no written language—and we work on piecing together names. It quickly turns silly, of course, once I scatter the letters and come up with the grand name of "Shoes." When "Hoes" comes up next, we both break into fits of giggles.

"Stop, stop," Josie breathes, clutching her stomach. "I'm going to pee all over myself laughing."

"I already did," I joke. "Can you imagine calling your kid Hoe? Everyone would just think it's another sa-khui name! 'Come sit with the tribe, Hoe. Go see your father, Hoe.'"

"Oh my god I caaaan't," Josie wail-giggles, and races for the bathroom.

Chortling, I swipe at the laughter-tears pouring from my eyes and mix the letters again and again, looking for the right combination. When Josie returns, I point out the newest combination. "What about Shae?" I pronounce it like "Shy" because of Haeden's name.

Josie's eyes widen. "Too close to Kae, but I do like Shae with the long A sound." She bites her lip. "I could even spell it as Shay...I mean, spelling doesn't matter when the sa-khui don't have a written language. You think anyone would give me shit for going off-brand?"

"It's your baby," I scold her. "You go off-brand as much as you like. Look at Anna and Elsa."

"I do like Shae," she says dreamily. "Or Shaena. That's pretty."

I do, too. "Talk to your mate, see what he thinks. I bet he likes it better than Zalah."

Josie smirks. "He'd like Hoe better than he'd like Zalah."

That sets us both into fits of giggles again.

"Mama!" a voice cries from outside, and both Josie and I perk up. Doesn't matter if it's your kid or not, the moment you hear the word "mama," your senses go on alert. In this case though, it really is my kid. Holvek's voice carries over the roofs. "Mama! Come and see what we've got!"

Josie and I exchange a look.

"Uh oh," Josie says, her mouth quirking. "That's not a good sign, Mama."

I fight back a groan. "No, it's not. Why do I have a feeling I'm going to be shown the biggest, ugliest dirtbeak ever?"

Josie laughs again, and her laughter cuts off. She sucks in a breath. "I think my water just broke. Might be time to find Haeden after all."

I squeeze her hand. "You sit down. I'll have Cashol go get him. Do you want the healer, too?"

"Not yet. I'm good for now, I think." She smiles up at me as she sits on her cushioned seat by the fire. "But Haeden is gonna want to see our daughter born."

"Say no more." I touch her shoulder, then move for the door. The moment I step outside, I see my mate, grinning with a mischievous look that tells me he's up to no good, and our son in front of him, an enormous grin just like his father's on his face, his arms filled with the longest-legged dvisti foal I've ever seen.

Ah, shit.

25

MEGAN

"Looks like you made a friend," I say to Holvek in my best mom voice, moving forward and ruffling my son's hair. "Before either of you say anything, Josie's having her baby and I need you to find Haeden," I say to Cashol. "He had Joha and Joden both with him, so he can't be far."

Cashol moves forward and quickly kisses my cheek. "We passed him on the trails a short time ago. I know where he was headed."

"Hurry, please. We can talk when you get back."

He winks at me—an expression he's picked up from being around me for so long—and then races back out of the canyon at full speed. I'm left with my son and a squirming, bleating dvisti colt. Holvek just radiates joy even as the thing poops in his arms.

Hoo boy.

I'm tempted to usher him back inside so we can sit with

Josie until Haeden returns, but I also don't want to bring an animal into the hut with us, not when she's about to give birth. I hesitate, and when I spot Kate nearby, I gesture for her to come over.

Her eyes grow wide at the sight of the little dvisti. "Oh my god, what a cute little guy!" She bends down so she's at eye-level with my son and the animal, beaming. "You must be so excited, Holvek."

"He's thrilled. Meanwhile, Josie's having her baby," I say quickly. "Can you sit with her until Haeden returns? I'm sorry to bother you, but I don't want to take this in to her hut." I gesture at the colt...who poops again.

"He's making fuel for us, Mama!" Holvek cries. "Isn't he wonderful?"

Kate stifles a laugh, and I force a smile to my face. "He's great, baby. Can you, Kate?"

"Of course." She chucks Holvek under the chin. "You go take care of your new friend...and maybe keep it away from Harrec. He's watching Mr. Fluffypuff right now."

Because Kate's "kitten" is growing bigger by the day and the snowcats eat dvisti. Right. "We'll be careful. Come on, baby." I put a hand on his back to steer him toward our hut and give Kate a grateful look. "Thank you. I owe you!"

She waves and ducks inside Josie's hut, and then I'm alone with my son. I debate for a moment to go and get the healer, but if Josie didn't want Maylak just yet, she knows best. I watch my son, his stout, boxy little body hustling as he heads toward our hut. Holvek is usually a stoic little thing, not a jokester like his daddy, or sarcastic like me. Sometimes I worry he's a little too serious for a child, but right now he's utterly radiant and all smiles as he reassures the bleating dvisti that everything's going to be all right, that they're going to be best friends.

I suspect I'm outvoted and we now have a new member of the family.

THERE ARE FAR TOO MANY THINGS FOR A DVISTI TO PEE AND POOP on in my tidy little house, but the hut behind us is empty and used for storage, so Holvek and I set up a little spot for the baby there. It's not as young as I thought upon second glance. He's small in stature but his legs are long, and he's growing the thick, gray bushy coat of a brutal season dvisti. It's got one twisted leg that looks like a genetic defect of some kind, and I'm guessing that's how my mate managed to find a colt and get it without bringing home the dead mother as meat.

The dvisti bleats and wails hungrily at Holvek until my sharp son goes and gets some roots from storage and feeds him bites of one. It tries to chew, but ends up spitting half of it on the ground, like it doesn't understand.

"You sit with him," I tell Holvek. "Mama will make you a root mash to feed him, okay?"

"Can I keep him?" Holvek asks in a hushed voice, his eyes so full of hope.

I'm going to kick Cashol's butt for putting me in this position. If I say no, I'm the bad parent. If I say yes…we have a damn dvisti. "I'll talk to your father," is all I say, but I know we have a new pet. I can see it in my son's radiant face. I smooth his messy hair back from his brow—just like his father's—and fight the urge to smother him to my chest and cuddle Holvek close. "You stay here and I'll be back soon enough."

"Can I sleep out here with him tonight?" Holvek asks. "I'll get some branches from the bushes and make him a nest so he can stay warm, but he's going to be so scared if he's alone. Please, Mama."

"You can if your father stays out here with you. You're too little otherwise." And I'm such a softie, because I know in a heartbeat that Cashol's going to camp out with his son while I make root mash all night.

Such a damn softie.

MEGAN

I'm chopping and dicing roots to add to the boiling water over the fire when the front door flap opens and Cashol ducks in.

"Did you find Haeden?" I turn back to my cutting, standing at the "kitchen" counter slab. "Is he back?"

"He was returning. I carried Joden and he carried Joha and we ran the entire way back." He comes up behind me and wraps his arms around my waist, nuzzling my neck. He's cold and icy all over, but his skin is flushed hot and sweaty, and I squirm out of his grasp. "What, you do not like wet kisses from your mate?"

"I like wet kisses," I grump. "Not sweat kisses."

Cashol laughs, then drops to his knees and wraps his arms around my waist, nuzzling my belly with the same attention. "I think your mother is mad at me, Casegan."

"I'm gonna be mad if his name is Casegan," I mutter. I'm not really mad, though. Just a little irked about the pet. "I'm going to feed our new little friend and then see if Josie needs anything." I glance over at him. "Okay with you if we watch Joden and Joha tonight? I imagine she can use the free time."

Cashol gets to his feet again and nibbles on my ear, and it's hard to stay mad at him, not when he's so damn handsy and affectionate. I pause in my root chopping and tilt my face up for a real kiss, and for a long moment, the world fades away and it's just me and my perfect, funny, exasperating, handsome mate, who kisses me as passionately as he did when we first resonated. "If Joden and Joha are here, I will not get to wake my pretty mate in the way she is accustomed."

I brush a sweaty lock of hair back from his brow. "You won't get to anyhow, because you're going to be staying out in the hut behind the house with our son, who wants to sleep with his new best friend."

"Caught in my own trap," Cashol says ruefully. He kisses me again. "I did not mean for it to happen, you know. We came across the dvisti tracks in the snow and I was showing Holvek how to follow them when we found the little one in the snow. She had been abandoned by her tribe for not being able to keep up. Did you see the leg?" He twists his hand, as if to demonstrate what I've already learned.

I nod, and apparently I'm a bigger softie than I knew, because just hearing that the colt was abandoned is enough for me. "You'll have to help Holvek set up a stable tomorrow. It can't stay in the house. Not unless we can train it not to relieve itself inside."

"Farli trained hers," Cashol muses. "I will talk with Salukh and Teef-nee and see what they suggest. Teef-nee is good with animals, yes?"

"Tiffany is good with everything," I agree. "And the dvisti is a girl?"

"It is. Very mild mannered and sweet. It tried to follow Holvek the moment it saw him."

Aw. My son must be so thrilled. I smile at that. I want my baby to be happy above all else, and if it means putting up with a pet, I'm gonna put up with a pet. "You should have seen the look on his face earlier. It was like the sun had come out. Do you think he's ready for all this responsibility?"

"I do," Cashol says seriously, and then rubs my belly. "It will keep him busy when our little treasure arrives."

Treasure. It's not the first time Cashol has told me that I'm his treasure...and it makes me think of names. I'm going to mull on that for a bit. "Will you finish making the root mash?" I ask my mate as he takes the knife from me and begins to cut. "I'll go get Joden and Joha."

He nods and leans over for a final kiss, and the movement is so easy and natural that it takes my breath away. I get to kiss this man every day of my life for the rest of my life and we're making beautiful children together.

God, I really am the luckiest. I kiss him back fiercely, stroke his back, and then head over to Josie's with a smile on my face.

HAEDEN IS MORE THAN HAPPY TO HAND THE CHILDREN OVER AS Josie spreads out the birthing mats, humming as if nothing in the world bothers her. Meanwhile, Haeden looks as disheveled and sweaty and off kilter as if he's the one giving birth. He hovers around Josie, offering her a cup of water, and I gather up Joha and a change of clothes, and entice energetic Joden with the idea of sleeping out in the storage hut with the new foal tonight.

Joden, the child hurricane, of course loves the idea and has ten thousand questions. I immediately put his jacket on him, hand him a snack, and send him over to Cashol and Holvek. Unlike her brother, Joha is a cuddly little joy of a child. She has fat chubby cheeks and Josie's little chin and a sweet—if noisy—

personality kind of like her mama. I get out Holvek's favorite toy when he was her age—colored bone shapes that fit into a carved box—and she spends most of the evening babbling to herself and pushing an orange peg into a round green hole. Definitely her mother (and her father's) kid. I busy myself with making hot broth drinks for the boys out in the "stable." Lukti joins them after Tiffany and Salukh stop by to offer tips, and then my poor mate is watching three boys and the dvisti and I feel just the teensiest bit sorry for him.

Holvek races in just before his regular bedtime to come give me a kiss, and I snuggle my boy before sending him back out with his father. "How is he doing? Your new friend?" I ask, worried that it might die on him and then we have to have a conversation about pets and death that I am *so* not ready to have. "Did he eat?"

"It's a girl, Mama." Holvek gives me an exasperated look that is entirely his father as I smooth his hair back. "Papa says it's a girl."

"Oh, I'm very sorry," I say solemnly. "Have you decided on a name?"

"Not yet. It has to be just the right name, Mama." His serious look returns. "Names are important."

"Yes they are." I give him one last hug. "Go on and rejoin your papa before Joden talks his ear off. I love you."

"I love you too, Mama!" He hugs me impulsively. "Thank you for letting me keep her."

My eyes fill with silly emotional tears. "Of course, baby. You know I love you."

"I know," he chirps at me, and then bounds back outside, and I feel like I was just handed some sort of Greatest Mom Award.

I curl up around Joha in the furs at bedtime, dreaming about baby names and treasures. Pearls. Jade. Ruby. Gold.

Silver. Jewels. *Jewel*, I muse as I smooth Joha's wispy hair back from her horn nubs. Maybe Jewel. I like that.

I must fall asleep, because when I wake up, the fire is nothing but coals and Cashol bends over the bed, stroking my face. I roll over, notice that Joha's still asleep, her thumb stuffed in her mouth, and keep my voice to a whisper. "Everything okay?"

Cashol nods, tracing my jaw with a tender caress. "Jo-see had her baby. A girl. She has named it Shae." He grins. "Strange name."

"It's a beautiful name," I say defensively. "How's she doing?"

"Haeden says it was the easiest birth yet, and Shae is the biggest of their three kits. Big and fat and entirely too big for someone as small as Jo-see to carry." He chuckles low. "We will keep Joden and Joha until later tomorrow, if that is all right."

"Of course," I murmur. "They need time to rest." We can keep them for weeks if needed. Josie's just right next door and I don't mind. I know she'll do the same for me when my baby comes. "How's Holvek?"

"Asleep with Thunder tucked safely under his arm. He is in love already."

I squint up at my mate in the darkness. "He named that shy little thing Thunder? After he told me it had to have the perfect name?"

Cashol chuckles. "You should have heard the noises it made when it smelled the root mash. She thundered at Holvek mightily until he fed her."

Thunder. I shake my head. Kids are weird. "Are you going back out there?"

He nods and his thumb skims over my lower lip. "I just wanted to check on my treasure. You know I do not like being apart from you. Not even this far."

My heart squeezes. "I love you."

"I love you as well." He gets up to leave, nothing but a shadow in the dim light of the house.

I grab his hand, thinking. "Wait. Speaking of names."

"Hmm?"

"How do you feel about Jewel? In my world, it's a type of treasure. I'd like to call our baby Jewel if it's a girl. What do you think?"

He smiles down at me. "I like it. I like everything you like."

"That's why we're perfect together," I whisper, yawning.

"Among many reasons. Now sleep, my mate. Tomorrow is a new day." He pulls the blankets higher around me and Joha, leans over and kisses my brow, and tends to the fire, stoking the coals just a little before heading back out to sleep in the stable with our son.

Jewel, I muse, touching my belly. Cashol, Megan, Holvek and Jewel. Oh, and Thunder. It sounds like a wonderful family to me. It's perfection.

Just like everything else in my life.

AUTHOR'S NOTE

Hello there!

It's taken us a while to swing back around to the Croatoan tribe, and for that, I apologize. There's a million stories floating around in my head right now (cue nervous laughter) and trying to juggle them all is sometimes a challenge. I've been wanting to write this one for a while, but the few times I've had the opportunity, Megan and Cashol didn't 'speak up'. It's funny, because I get the most ideas for characters when other stories are talking loudly. These two started talking again while I was writing the most recent Fireblood Dragons book and so I decided to roll right into their story once that one was done.

Like Marlene's story, this one is a bit 'lower conflict'. It's been established that Megan was pretty much a homebody ever since arriving on the planet, so that limited the scope of their particular tale. I couldn't exactly send them trekking all over the planet to have adventures, but I'm also surprisingly okay with that? Because I also like the smaller stories. It allows me to 'hang out' in the cave a bit more, and in this case, show the friendship between Josie and Megan.

Megan also had some issues to work through with the loss of her pregnancy and the effect it would have on her when she's thrust into a world where she perceives her greatest value is her ability to get pregnant again. Naturally her and Josie would feel anxious at not resonating right away since so many people did, and that anxiety would lead to an obsessive amount of people-pleasing. It's like when you hear your job is about to let someone go...you find yourself working harder and volunteering for shitty work just to show what a valuable asset you are.

Luckily for her, Cashol is far more easy-going. He really tries to give Megan the space he thinks she needs...which only makes things worse. Megan doesn't need - or want - space. She wants someone she can cling to with all her might so she can be reassured they're always there for her. We all need different things in relationships, and the best pairings are on the same page, emotionally. Cashol's happy to be clung to, after losing everyone in his family. He likes being needed (who doesn't?) and so both of them get what they need in the other partner.

This means we're down to one last story in Ice Planet Barbarians before I officially have 'run out' of romances to tell. I'll do Nora and Dagesh's story (hopefully sometimes this year) but I don't know if this means we'll jump ahead in the timeline or we'll do a second round of stories (like the honeymoons but longer) or what. I'm reluctant to leave these characters behind, but I'm also reluctant to mess up the happy ever afters I've given them. So we shall see!

After this, we're heading back to Icehome. There's a lot brewing on the beach and I feel like it's going to come to a head in Mari and T'chai's book and that will have some interesting consequences for how things unfold in Icehome for a while.

Also I am dying (dying!) to write my Corsair books but as usual, my schedule is brim-full and I'm trying to work everything in. My goal is to tackle a little bit of everything for the rest of the year unless the characters drag me in a totally different direction. Who knows! The good news is I'm not stopping anytime soon.

(That might also be bad news, depending on how far behind you are on your reading.)

<3
Much Love,
Ruby

THE PEOPLE OF ICE PLANET BARBARIANS

At Croatoan

Mated Couples and their kits

Vektal (Vehk-tall) – The chief of the sa-khui. Mated to Georgie.

Georgie – Human woman (and unofficial leader of the human females). Has taken on a dual-leadership role with her mate. Currently pregnant with her third kit.

Talie (Tah-lee) – Their first daughter.

Vekka (Veh-kah) – Their second daughter.

Maylak (May-lack) – Tribe healer. Mated to Kashrem.

Kashrem (Cash-rehm) - Her mate, also a leather-worker.

Esha (Esh-uh) – Their teenage daughter.

Makash (Muh-cash) — Their younger son.

Sevvah (Sev-uh) – Tribe elder, mother to Aehako, Rokan, and Sessah

Oshen (Aw-shen) – Tribe elder, her mate

Sessah (Ses-uh) - Their youngest son (currently at Icehome beach)

Ereven (Air-uh-ven) Hunter, mated to Claire.
Claire – Mated to Ereven
Erevair (Air-uh-vair) - Their first child, a son
Relvi (Rell-vee) – Their second child, a daughter

Liz – Raahosh's mate and huntress. Currently at Icehome beach.
Raahosh (Rah-hosh) – Her mate. A hunter and brother to Rukh. Currently at Icehome beach.
Raashel (Rah-shel) – Their daughter.
Aayla (Ay-lah) – Their second daughter
Ahsoka (Ah-so-kah) - Their third daughter.

Stacy – Mated to Pashov. Unofficial tribe cook.
Pashov (Pah-showv) – son of Kemli and Borran, brother to Farli, Zennek, and Salukh. Mate of Stacy. Currently at Icehome beach.
Pacy (Pay-see) – Their first son.
Tash (Tash) – Their second son.

Nora – Mate to Dagesh. Currently pregnant after a second resonance.
Dagesh (Dah-zhesh) (the g sound is swallowed) – Her mate. A hunter.
Anna & Elsa – Their twin daughters.

Harlow – Mate to Rukh. Once 'mechanic' to the Elders' Cave. Currently at Icehome beach.
Rukh (Rookh) – Former exile and loner. Original name Maarukh. (Mah-rookh). Brother to Raahosh. Mate to Harlow. Father to Rukhar. Currently at Icehome beach.

Rukhar (Roo-car) – Their son.
Daya (dye-uh) - Their daughter.

Megan – Mate to Cashol. Mother to Holvek. Pregnant.
Cashol (Cash-awl) – Mate to Megan. Hunter. Father to Holvek.
Holvek (Haul-vehk) – their son. Has a pet, Thunder, an orphaned dvisti colt with a twisted leg.

Marlene (Mar-lenn) – Human mate to Zennek. French.
Zennek (Zehn-eck) – Mate to Marlene. Father to Zalene. Brother to Pashov, Salukh, and Farli. Currently at Icehome beach.
Zalene (Zah-lenn) – daughter to Marlene and Zennek.

Ariana – Human female. Mate to Zolaya. Basic school 'teacher' to tribal kits.
Zolaya (Zoh-lay-uh) – Hunter and mate to Ariana. Father to Analay & Zoari.
Analay (Ah-nuh-lay) – Their son.
Zoari (Zoh-air-ee) - Their newborn daughter.

Tiffany – Human female. Mated to Salukh. Tribal botanist.
Salukh (Sah-luke) – Hunter. Son of Kemli and Borran, brother to Farli, Zennek, and Pashov. Currently at Icehome beach.
Lukti (Lookh-tee) – Their son.

Aehako (Eye-ha-koh) – Mate to Kira, father to Kae. Son of Sevvah and Oshen, brother to Rokan and Sessah.
Kira – Human woman, mate to Aehako, mother of Kae. Was the first to be abducted by aliens and wore an ear-translator for a long time. Recently re-resonated to her mate a 2nd time.
Kae (Ki –rhymes with 'fly') – Their daughter.

===

Kemli (Kemm-lee) – Female elder, mother to Salukh, Pashov, Zennek, and Farli. Tribe herbalist.

Borran (Bore-awn) – Her mate, elder. Tribe brewer.

===

Josie – Human woman. Mated to Haeden.

Haeden (Hi-den) – Hunter. Previously resonated to Zalah, but she died (along with his khui) in the khui-sickness before resonance could be completed. Now mated to Josie.

Joden (Joe-den) – Their first child, a son.

Joha (Joe-hah) – Their second child, a daughter.

Shae (Shay, rhymes with play) - Their third child, a newborn daughter.

===

Rokan (Row-can) – Oldest son to Sevvah and Oshen. Brother to Aehako and Sessah. Adult male hunter. Now mated to Lila. Has 'sixth' sense.

Lila – Maddie's sister. Once hearing impaired, recently reacquired on *The Tranquil Lady* via med bay. Resonated to Rokan.

Rollan (Row-lun) – Their first child, a son.

Lola (nicknamed Lolo) - Their recently born daughter.

===

Hassen (Hass-en) – Hunter. Previously exiled. Mated to Maddie. Currently at Icehome beach.

Maddie – Lila's sister. Found in second crash. Mated to Hassen.

Masan (Mah-senn) – Their son. Owns a baby dirtbeak named Millicent.

===

Asha (Ah-shuh) – Mate to Hemalo. Mother to Hashala (deceased) and Shema.

Hemalo (Hee-muh-low) – Mate to Asha. Father to Hashala (deceased) and Shema.

Shema (Shee-muh) – Their daughter.

Farli – (Far-lee) Adult daughter to Kemli and Borran. Her brothers are Salukh, Zennek, and Pashov. She has a pet dvisti named Chompy (Chahm-pee). Mated to Mardok. Pregnant. Currently at Icehome beach.

Mardok (Marr-dock) – Bron Mardok Vendasi, from the planet Ubeduc VII. Arrived on *The Tranquil Lady*. Mechanic and ex-soldier. Resonated to Farli and elected to stay behind with the tribe. Currently at Icehome beach.

Bek – (Behk) – Hunter. Brother to Maylak. Mated to Elly.

Elly – Former human slave. Kidnapped at a very young age and has spent much of life in a cage or enslaved. First to resonate amongst the former slaves brought to Not-Hoth. Mated to Bek. Pregnant.

Harrec (Hair-ek) – Hunter. Squeamish. Also a tease. Recently resonated to Kate.

Kate – Human female. Extremely tall & strong, with white-blonde curly hair. Recently resonated to Harrec. Pregnant.

Mr. Fluffypuff aka Puff/Poof - Her orphaned snowcat kitten.

Warrek (War-ehk) – Tribal hunter and teacher. Son to Eklan (now deceased). Resonated to Summer.

Summer – Human female. Tends to ramble in speech when nervous. Chess aficionado. Recently resonated to Warrek.

Taushen (Tow – rhymes with cow – shen) – Hunter. Recently mated to Brooke. Experiencing a happiness renaissance. Currently at Icehome beach.

Brooke – Human female with fading pink hair. Former hairdresser, fond of braiding the hair of anyone that walks close enough. Mated to Taushen and recently pregnant. Currently at Icehome beach.

Vaza (Vaw-zhuh) – Widower and elder. Loves to creep on the ladies. Currently pleasure-mated with Gail and at Icehome beach. Adopted father to Z'hren.

Gail – Divorced older human woman. Had a son back on Earth (deceased). Approx fiftyish in age. Pleasure-mated with Vaza, adopted mother to Z'hren.

Unmated Elders

Drayan (Dry-ann) – Elder.

Drenol (Dree-nowl) – Elder. Friend to Lukti.

Vadren (Vaw-dren) – Elder. Sometimes bedmate to Kemli and Borran.

WANT MORE TO READ?

You're home. You're bored. You've watched *Tiger King* twenty times already. Why not binge on some Kindle Unlimited reads? My entire backlist is available to borrow, which means you can dig in and escape the world for just a little while.

Need a suggestion?

Start Ice Planet Barbarians from the beginning!

Ice Planet Barbarians

Barbarian Alien

Escape to another world with some slow-burn epic fantasy romance.

Bound to the Battle God

Sworn to the Shadow God

Something shorter and sweeter (but still with aliens!)

When She's Ready

When She's Married

Pretty Human

The Alien's Mail-Order Bride